The Glue Ponys

CHRIS WILSON

THE GLUE PONYS

A TANGERINE PRESS PUBLICATION

ISBN 978-1-910691-15-1 (paperback)
      978-1-910691-14-4 (hardback)

THE GLUE PONYS. COPYRIGHT © 2016 CHRIS WILSON
FIRST PUBLISHED 2016 BY TANGERINE PRESS
18 RIVERSIDE ROAD
GARRATT BUSINESS PARK
LONDON
SW17 0BA
ENGLAND
eatmytangerine.com
PRINTED & BOUND IN ENGLAND BY CLAYS LTD

Printed on acid-free paper

Acknowledgements

Some of these stories first appeared in *Not Shut Up* magazine and the limited edition chapbook *The Tree & Two More* (Sick Fly Publications, 2016). The author and publisher are particularly grateful to Rachel Dyer for editing these stories. Thanks are also due to: Thomas Rees for inspiration with the original 'ponys' vision; Agata Cardoso; Gareth McConnell; John Gladdy for the photographs; Marek Kazmierski; Zach Sebastian; Alex King for his input; Wayne Hanson. This book was published with the assistance of Arts Council England.

Table of Contents

This is a book about the broken and discarded, the lost and the wandering of America, with whom I shared some moments on the way to the abattoir.

—CW

The Glue Ponys

The Lieutenant

When lieutenant Teddy Malovich finally died they left him in the bed for a week and then put his body inside some black plastic trashcan liners, wrapped it up with duct tape and put him in the hallway closet. He didn't weigh much, but they had to fold him so his knees tucked up beneath his chin and lay him on his side underneath the jackets and shirts and Japanese kimonos that hung from the clothes rail in order to get the door to close.

They were the last of his children, all the others were either dead or in prison in the jungles of northern Thailand, or else kneeling down on the dust streets of Kathmandu dressed in rags, begging change from tourists so that they could buy a little more heroin.

For the past two years Sean and Deedee had been looking after the lieutenant as he lay dying in his bed, washing his long, thin hair, spoon-feeding him pureed carrots and mashed potatoes and shooting him up with his favourite mixture of speed, PCP and Dilaudid.

Every now and then they'd try to have a party and put on their platform boots and do their makeup and go out to Polk Street and bring back some young kid who didn't mind taking off his clothes and dancing around the bed-room naked to some old Eartha Kitt voodoo song and then curling up in the bed next to the lieutenant so that he could hold them gently like a teddy bear and ask them what their name was and then run a long, thin finger along the outside of their lips after they'd said it.

All the jewelry was gone, all the fur coats and Persian carpets and silver goblets cast out of human skulls in Benares had long past the expiration dates on the pawn tickets that sat in the kitchen drawers. The only money left came from the VA checks and social security payments that arrived once a month in the letterbox downstairs.

Lieutenant Teddy Malovich had been the tank com-mander of an M48 Patton in the armored cavalry at twenty one years of age and had come out of two tours of Vietnam with multiple decorations for courageous action under fire, a monstrous heroin habit and a deep desire to make and dwell in an alternative universe where the men could be girls and the girls could be anything they wanted to be.

So that's what he'd done; he'd ordained himself as the jade tiger empress of the underworld and created a planet for his children to play in, funded by the proceeds of a chemical formula for making angel dust that his college roommate had given him just before he had committed suicide. The PCP went out and the heroin came back from the four corners of the globe, transported by his little army of drag queens and runaways and self-harming anorexic pornstars. And then everybody died, or just about everybody, and the birthday parties under a full moon in Kovalam or dancing around the pyramids became more sober affairs, conducted with syringes in a Haight Street safe house where the last of the few gathered to pay homage to the lieutenant as he turned to dust in the silk sheets of his bed.

Sean and Deedee cashed the checks, the lieutenant signed them on the back and they'd walk down to the liquor store holding hands and pass them over the counter to Fat Joe and come back with just enough money for the lieutenant to pay the rent and the bills and their methadone scripts for the month and get the lieutenant his cases of Ensure fortified dietary supplement drinks and his cans of carrots and new potatoes and then ten cartons of Marlboro's and that was it, the shopping was done, and what little cash that was left over was theirs.

When the first check arrived after the lieutenant had been wrapped in plastic and secured in the hallway closet, Sean had opened it up and got out a pad of yellow stick-ons and started practicing the lieutenant's signature, and when it looked about right he signed it on the back and put on an old lace wedding dress and a pair of steel toe combat boots and gone down to the liquor store and cashed it. Deedee stayed at home because she was scared, but when Sean returned with a big bag of heroin and a big bag of crystal meth she figured maybe everything was going to be alright after all, and it was for a while, because nobody knew the lieutenant was dead but them.

Sean and Deedee didn't pay the rent, they were just children – thirty year old runaways who'd always been looked after by someone or another since they could remember. They didn't know how to pay the rent or the bills, that's what the lieutenant had done. He'd taken care of everything and they loved him and he loved them, but now that he was dead they couldn't figure out anything much further ahead than the next shot and then the next one, and when the eviction notice came and the gas and the electricity were cut off and the landlord started coming around and knocking on the door, they sat quietly on the carpet in the living room with their syringes in their hands, hoping that everyone would just go away and leave them alone, but they didn't, and on the morning that the front door was kicked down and the bailiffs came up the stairs covering their noses with their hands and saying, 'Jesus, what the fuck is that smell?' Sean and Deedee realized that they were going to have to find somebody else to look after them; the lieutenant couldn't do it anymore.

The bailiffs put everything out on the street: the bed, the dining room table and chairs, the boxes of books and old LPs and carrier bags full of clothes. They even put the lieutenant out on the street in his duct-taped plastic coffin and when the truck pulled up and they started throwing everything into the back of it, Sean and Deedee sat on the curb and watched, smoking cigarettes and crying, because the lieutenant was really gone and there weren't going to be any more checks or any more parties and the world seemed to be a scarier place somehow. When the truck closed up its doors and started its engine and headed out to the Bay View dump Sean and Deedee got up slowly and wiped their noses with the back of their hands and started off down the hill.

The Freeway

She didn't know if she was drunk or dying. There was a fire burning about three feet in front of her face and on the other side through the flames she thought she could make out a pair of old cowboy boots and next to them a big black dog on a chain that was staring at her through the fire and growling. She tried to push herself up from the ground, but her arms were shaking and there was no strength left anywhere inside her, so she gave up and just let her face fall back into the dirt.

As she lay there with her eyes closed she tried to remember what she was doing here and what had happened and where here was and why the fuck nobody had tried to help her when she'd been screaming so loud. It was all broken up, the faces and the voices and the pain between her legs.

She came to in the morning and the fire was out and the dog was gone and she stood up slowly and gathered up her clothes that were lying about in different places along the trash-strewn ditch that was dug out of the bank that ran along the edge of the freeway. She could hear the cars and the trucks going by just above on the other side of the fence line, some of them were going so fast that the trees above her head seemed to rock and sway in the air from the gusts that they left in their wake.

When she had gathered up her clothes she sat on a cinder block and pulled on her jeans and buttoned up the two buttons that were left on her blouse and put her feet inside her sneakers and laced them up. She couldn't find her panties or her socks and she remembered that she'd left her bra in some man's truck three days ago now. She'd kept thinking she would buy another one but she hadn't got around to it yet.

When she was dressed she stood up and swept her hair back and tied it in a bunch on the back of her head using a piece of wire she found on the ground to hold it in place, then she spat on her hands and tried to clean some of the dirt and the blood from her forearms and neck but she ran out of spit and there wasn't any water to be found so she gave up and started scrambling up the side of the bank that led to the chain link fence at the edge of the asphalt on her hands and knees.

When she got to the fence she started walking down the line looking for holes that had been cut through the links that she could crawl through but she couldn't find any. After a while she stopped and looked up at the row of razor wire that ran ten feet high along the top of the fence. Further down on the right she could see an old duffel jacket that was lying on top of the blades. She thought if she could just climb up there maybe she could use the jacket as padding and pull herself over and drop down on the other side, but when she got up there she cut her hands badly and the blades came through the jacket and ripped into her stomach and her thighs, but she gritted her teeth and kept going and when she managed to get a grip on the other side of the fence, she held tight with her cut hands and flipped her legs up and over the top and came tumbling down and landed on her side at the edge of the freeway.

She lay still for a while and got up her strength. They were going too fast, the cars and the trucks and the motorcycles and there was no room for them to stop, so when she rose she walked on the edge of the slow lane for about two miles until she came to a lay by and she turned around to face the traffic and then it happened. She started shaking and her knees buckled in and she bent over and got sick and her head was spinning and it all came back to her, everything, from as far back as she could remember. But there was another part of her, way down somewhere inside, that just wasn't going to let her break and it held her and it lifted up her chin so that her eyes met with the eyes of the drivers coming down the freeway and she raised her right arm into the air with her fingers balled up in a fist and stuck her thumb straight up and into the heart of the blue morning sky.

The Pugilist

Shorty walked like a gimp – his right leg went up and his toe pointed up in the air and then he brought it down and when his heel hit the ground his whole body jerked forward and then he'd do it again with his left leg and that was how he walked.

He was a little white fucker with a bald head and shitty tattoos. He was cut pretty good though and he liked to tell people how he was the Nebraska State bantamweight boxing champion when he was in high school. Most people didn't care much unless they were thinking about fighting him and then they wondered.

So I said, 'How come you walk like that, Shorty?'

And he looked at me like he was weighing up the distance for his left jab then said, 'Ah, the fuckin' Mexicans stabbed me four times in my ass down on Mission and I didn't go to the hospital, just wrapped it up with bandages and went to sleep and when I woke up this is how I walked.'

For a while we played spades together and he could count every card that had been played. He always made his bid but if anyone looked at him wrong or laughed accidentally he would throw all his cards in the air, pick up the scoring pencil like it was a screwdriver, jump up on the table and make his little speech. 'My name's Shorty Moran and I done five state prison terms with three different numbers and I'll kill anyone who fuckin' says another word, got it?' Usually people got it and they'd shrug and nod their heads and he'd jump down from the table and pick up his cards and put them back in suit and then he'd sit down and say, 'Whose play is it? Come on man, let's do this fuckin' thing, let's play some spades!' After a while nobody wanted to play with us anymore and I didn't blame them. Shorty would come over to my bunk and say, 'Come on London, let's get a game, I'm fuckin' bored.' And I'd sigh and get up slowly.

And then one day I said, 'Listen Shorty nobody wants to play with you 'cos you're a fuckin' asshole.'

And he looked at me all crazy for a second and said, 'What the fuck did you say?' And I looked right back and said, 'You're a fuckin' asshole.'

Well Shorty stood there real still, then he raised his hands up slow like the bell had rang and just stared into his hands for a while and then he started to cry. I mean he really cried – he just stood there with the snot running down his chin and his little chest heaving out 'boo hoo hoo hoo' and all the Mexicans started looking down out of their bunks and the whole cell got quiet and then Little Smurf from East Palo Alto started to laugh and that was it – forty eight Mexicans threw back their heads and laughed with joy and pointed their fingers at the spot on the floor where Shorty was falling apart.

'Shorty, stop crying man,' I said. 'What the fuck is wrong with you? You're really fuckin' up, you seriously need to stop crying man, this is not good. Shorty, stop fuckin' crying!' But it was no use, Shorty was gone and the next thing I knew the Mexicans were jumping down from their bunks and gathering in a circle around the spot where Shorty used to be.

I can tell they're hungry and fucking hate his guts then one old loco from Sinaloa does a big hawk and pulls up a green lugi from the depths and spits it on Shorty's face and they're still for a second to see what might happen but Shorty just keeps on sobbing and that's it, they go crazy and they're spitting and swearing and someone kicks him in the back and he goes down and they go down with him and start punching him on the head and ripping his jump-suit and Shorty's not doing anything about it and I think, oh no, this is all too fucking weird, and I try to pull some of them off him but they turn on me and pin me to the wall and say, 'Calmate juero este loco es muerto.'

I don't know how long it took for the cops to push the alarm and come storming in with their batons and shields and tear gas and start clubbing Mexicans and pulling them off what was left of Shorty but however long it had been, for Shorty it was too long. But then again I had this feel-ing that Shorty knew exactly what he was doing and it was all timed to perfection because he was fucking dead and that had been what he was thinking about when he'd been staring at the place where his boxing gloves used to be, that place on his knuckles where both hands had 'love' and 'hate' tattooed across them.

So they had some little investigation but the Mexicans had covered the cameras with towels and everyone swore he just fell out of his bunk, and Shorty was a nobody like the rest of us. After a week of lockdown they let it lay and I got a new spade partner with a bit more etiquette and ground out my little six months in that shit-fuck tank in San Mateo county jail. Oh yeah he really was, I mean, when I think about it, Shorty was a fucking asshole.

The Glue Ponys

Larry was the first to wake up. It was raining again and with the fever he couldn't figure out if he was boiling or freezing. His few remaining teeth were bouncing a tattoo off each other as his jaw played out the rhythm of the infection. He groaned and sat up in the green army sleeping bag and spat out some blood, he sucked in his cheeks and pulled up another mouthful from his swollen gums and spat that out too.

The tarpaulin was sagging in the middle. He would have to get up and pull one of the sides tight to empty the pool that was gathering or the whole thing would come down on their heads. He reached over to his black down vest and took out his straight shooter and pusher and lit his Bic lighter and held the flame low under the cracked black glass tube and ran it up and down to wet any resin that might be left, then put his pusher in one end and twisting his wrist worked the Brillo up the tube and started again from the other side. After three times he exhaled and turned up the lighter to full and drew a long sad hit to get him up and moving.

The abscess had reached from his collarbone to the

bottom of his jaw on the left side of his neck. He had to hold his head still or it would start leaking down the inside of his T-shirt and when it dried it would glue the fabric to his skin. He didn't want to go to the hospital again, it was a long walk and he'd have to push his cart with everything in it and today he just didn't have the strength.

There were three of them at the campsite: Jonesy, Holly and him. He'd been with Jonesy for two years now and Holly had been coming and going for most of that time. She was a good girl – she didn't hook or turn people over, she ran credits and pushed her own cart for bottles and cans and if you were sick she'd do you a cotton as long as you paid her back when she needed it. Jonesy was the Levi's man – he hit up all the charity stores and vintage boutiques on Castro and could come out with ten pairs at a time. There was a place on Valencia that paid cash for second-hand Levi's then sent them to Japan in bulk lots. Jonesy was from Miami and as black as the tar on the freeway. Larry hated niggers but Jonesy was the best friend he'd ever had. Not that he'd tell him, with Jonesy you didn't have to speak too much, you just got on with what needed to be done.

It had started as cotton fever, which was no big deal, everybody got it now and then from a dirty hit, but with him it came with every shot he did. At SF General they'd run some tests and x-rays and the doctor had said, 'Well, I'm afraid you have severe endocarditis, which means you have an infection in your heart valves from foreign substances being introduced. The next time you inject yourself could be your last and I'm not exaggerating, you're a very sick man'. Larry had nodded his head, picked up his prescription at the hospital pharmacy, gone back to the campsite, put three cottons in his cooker that Jonesy had left for him and hit himself in the neck. That's when the abscess began.

At ten o'clock they were all up and fixed and they packed the carts for the long walk to the Sisters on Potrero. It was a Sunday, the hardest day of the week except for Christmas, so on Sundays they went to the Sisters and ate stew and loaded up on stale sandwiches and pudding cups and had a shower if they could be bothered.

By Harrison, Larry was flagging. Jonesy kept looking over his shoulder waiting for him to catch up and he'd start off again. He didn't say a word but he was there. When they got to the Sisters breakfast was over, but Holly had saved them each a bowl of soup and two boiled eggs. They sat on the wooden benches in the courtyard and waited for them to bring out some clean socks and candy bars.

Holly opened her tin of butts and rolled them three smokes and looked over at Larry.

'Man, your neck's fucked up. It stinks and your cheeks are turning purple. Larry, do you hear me man?'

'I hear you.'

'So what the fuck are you gonna do?'

Larry took a hit on the roll up and looked up to the clouds and said: 'I'm gonna wait 'till it gets better.'

'It's not gonna get better, man, it's gonna get a whole lot worse you ignorant fuck, and me and Jonesy gotta worry about you and you're slowing us down.'

'So move on,' said Larry and closed his eyes.

The campsite was under the concrete pylons of the Van Ness on-ramp that ran into 80 to the Bay Bridge or 101 going south. It had a cyclone fence that ringed in the west and the north, behind which were some old auto-wrecking yards and dead-end alleys leading off Mission. The only way in was from the east through the ice plants that circled the copse of oak and eucalyptus trees that had served as a sanctuary for the drifters and winos and street junkies ever since the freeway had been built. There were rats all over the place – sometimes Jonesy would take the machete that he kept in his cart and go on a rampage but it didn't seem much use. They just ate their own dead and came back fatter and meaner. When it rained the whole place turned to mud and if the carts were loaded down with bottles and cans and bits of scrap metal they had to use pieces of plywood and corrugated cardboard to put under the wheels to get them moving again. The cops pretty much left them alone; that's why they were here. 'Home sweet home,' Larry would say when they came back after scoring, 'everybody needs a home, even old glue ponies like us.' And Jonesy would just nod his head.

Jonesy was tall and wide and thin at the same time, like wire cables bound tight. His fists were two hammers and his nose had been broken so many times that it whistled as he breathed. Once when Holly had been crying about the little boy she'd left with her mother Jonesy had said, 'I got five kids and a wife in Tallahassee I ain't seen for near ten years. They're better off without me and most likely your boy's the same.' That was the only thing Jonesy ever said about himself and deep down Holly knew he was right.

When Jonesy fixed all he did was roll up his right pant leg – he had a hole in the soft skin behind his knee there like a well that never ran dry. He used ten-mil syringes that he dug out of the garbage bags outside veterinary hospitals because they were the only ones that were long enough now to reach the bottom of the well. It hadn't dried yet but each day it got deeper and deeper.

The next morning when they got up to start again Larry stayed in his sleeping bag. He was tired. 'I'm so fuckin' tired,' he said. In some ways he thought the abscess was a good thing. There wasn't much of him left. I'm already a ghost, he thought and looked down at his hands which had been covered over the years in a hundred tattoos of skulls and upside-down crosses and the names of prisons he'd lived in and women that he'd beaten and children that he'd walked away from and he wondered what it had all been about.

When the ambulance came Jonesy stood on the sidewalk where the ice plants began and watched. Holly was long gone, she had wanted to bury him at the campsite, but Jonesy said no and walked down to the pay phone on Shotwell Street and dialed 911. He was surprised to see the cost of a phonecall had gone up to twenty cents. It had always been a dime, but then he remembered that he hadn't made a phone call in a long while.

The Braces

She had little piggy eyes and dry frizzled brown hair held
back in a ponytail. She was sitting up straight on the brown
vinyl couch in a black bikini with her hands held together
on her lap like she was praying, waiting for instructions.
She was scared and excited at the same time and small
beads of sweat glistened like tears on her white temples.

'Now Jennifer,' said the director, 'when I say "rolling"
Tommy here's gonna knock on the door and you're gonna
get up and walk over and say "who is it?" and he's gonna
say "it's the plumber" and you're gonna say "ok" and then
let him in, got it?' She nodded her head and tried to smile,
her teeth were encaged in a silver mass of braces with small
rubber bands interspersed half an inch apart all the way
around her mouth. 'Good,' said the director. 'Now when
he comes in the door take him into the kitchen and tell him
how the sink's all blocked up and then lean over to turn on
the faucet and stick your ass right out, yeah? Stick your
ass right out and kinda point it at him and roll it slowly
around, ok?'

'Ok,' she said, concentrating hard so she could
remember.

'Now Tommy here's gonna put down his toolbox and lean up against your ass with his crotch and reach his hand over and put it on top of your hand on the tap and I want you to leave the tap running, remember that, yeah? I want the tap running when he fucks you.' She nodded her head again but then slowly put up her hand like she was in the classroom and suddenly had a really important question to ask.

'Yeah?' said the director.

'Well,' she said, 'well I thought the sink was blocked up so won't it just get overflowed?'

'Jennifer,' said the director, trying to be patient, 'honey, the sink's not blocked up we're just pretending, yeah? We are making a fuckin' movie Jennifer and for fuck's sake, take those rubber bands out of your mouth so you can suck Tommy's cock after he's fucked you.' Her cheeks flushed pink and she lowered her eyes then walked over to where her bag was on the orange shagpile carpet by the couch and rummaged through its contents until her hand emerged with the white plastic container that she used for her brace bands. She reached her thumbnail into her mouth and unhooked each rubber band from its place on the wires that ran around her teeth and gently placed them into the container and then put the lid back on it and sat it on top of her bag. She rolled her jaw around to loosen it up and then turned back around to the director and said, 'Ok, I'm ready.'

'Good,' said the director and clapped his hands twice in the air above his head, 'let's make this fuckin' movie.'

The Bus Stop

Mark Laffollett got hit by a school bus when he was fourteen years old and it changed his life forever. His brother Mike was a hood and Paul probably would have been a hood himself, but now everything he did was in slow motion.

'Iiiii nnnneeeddd aaa llliiiigghhttt,' Mark would say to the kids down by the first log in the trees behind the rec center, and someone would give him a pack of matches and he'd pull out his brass hash pipe from his jacket pocket. Then he'd take out a rubber hose from his other pocket and undo his belt buckle, pull down his pants and slowly squat down, sticking one end of the hose right up his butt. Then he'd load his pipe, strike a match, take a big hit and pick up the other end of the hose and blow all the smoke straight up his ass. If his brother Mike was there nobody said much, but if he wasn't, one of the girls would usually say something like, 'Oh my god that's fuckin' gross why are you doing that?' and Mark would do his slow laugh and say, 'Iii wwwaaannnttt tttooo gggeeettt hhhiiiggghh,' and then offer them his hash pipe, which usually set off some deep thinking as the girl tried to figure out if the stem of the hash pipe had actually been anywhere near his asshole or not.

Mark hung out with Tommy Patton who'd been his best friend since they were in kindergarten. Tommy Patton's dad was a dentist and he was one of the two black men in the San Mateo Highlands. Tommy's mom was a pretty blonde lady who drove a silver Karmann Ghia until one night she drove it up to San Francisco, parked it, and then jumped off the Golden Gate Bridge. Tommy had two hawks and an eagle that lived in a big wire mesh cage in his back garden. I don't think they ever came out; they were just there. Tommy sold pot and hash and speed and acid and sherm and always wore a black wooly beanie pulled low over his forehead. He had sex with a lot of the white girls in the neighborhood and if the other guys had a problem with that they didn't say much because Tommy could fight. Tommy had an older brother who went to university. Tommy didn't go to university. He went to prison.

Sometimes in the morning Mark would show up at the bus stop where the other kids were hanging out smoking cigarettes and rolling joints, waiting for the bus to take them to school. The bus pulled up and all the kids got on, and as it drove away they looked out the back window and saw Mark rocking slowly from side to side on his own, trying to figure out what was happening.

In the summer of '76 somebody started trying to set fire to the houses on Tarrytown Street where Mark lived. None of them really got burned badly – a few mailboxes got torched and a couple of doors were singed from ripped up newspaper that had been placed on them and set alight.

It didn't take long for the police to figure out what was happening because they saw Mark walking slowly up the street when they arrived, heading to the bus stop to wait for the kids to get back from school. I think they sent him to Atascadero State mental hospital after that. I bet you he's still there thirty years later, walking slowly around the wards, looking for the bus stop and a light.

I saw Tommy Patton twenty years on in Redwood City jail. He didn't have his beanie, but he hadn't changed much, other than that he was facing charges because his three-year-old son had found an ounce of cocaine in a cupboard and eaten it and died, so they were trying to hit him with negligent homicide. I said, 'Hey Tommy,' as I was going by in shackles heading to court, but he didn't seem to recognise me. It's ok, I thought to myself – it was a long time ago and there wasn't much to speak about anyway, just the usual bullshit of growing up in American suburbia.

The Dreamer

Dead John was called Dead John because that's what was tattooed on the fingers of his hands just above the knuckles. The left one said DEAD and the right one said JOHN, so that's who he was.

He'd hooked up with the youngster in Monterey where they were sleeping under the pier and the kid was just starting out on the short-term career of a male hustler, working the cars up and down the pier and the naval officers from down near Fort Ord.

'Boy, you won't make no money down here,' Dead John had said, 'you need to get up to Frisco to make any dough, yeah?' And the kid had shrugged his shoulders and said, 'I don't know where it is,' and Dead John had said, 'Well I'll take ya, you just gotta keep me well when we get there, yeah?' And the kid had shrugged his shoulders again and said, 'Ok then.'

'Of all the places I ever been this one's gotta be the worst. Yup,' said Dead John later on the first night when they'd given up after only making forty five miles and he hawked up a ball of brown shit from the bottom of his chest and chewed on it a bit, then spat it into the sad flicker of a fire, over which his wet socks were dangling, speared on the end of a wire coat hanger that he'd opened up to cook the hot dogs they'd stolen from the 7-Eleven across the street from the field. Dead John moaned a lot. Not a nice kind of moaning with humour or life, more like a worn metal brake that had burned up all the rubber and just grated sparks.

'People round here would rather shoot ya than give ya a dime or a ride,' he said, rocking backwards and forwards squatted down on his bare heels. 'Twelve hours spent standin' in the fuckin' rain and we made two dollars and twenty two cents and no fuckin' ride, thank you very much, two dollars and twenty two mothafuckin' pissant centavos, eh?' Then he started laughing as sour thunder-heads of steam rose up from the cotton fibers of his socks. 'I tell you what boy, we gotta get outta Watsonville tomorrow, we gotta pick up early and see if we can't catch something north fast, this place is no good for anyone but Mexicans. Yup, white trash is about as welcome as niggers in this fuckin' town.' When the socks were done he sat back and pulled them over his mottled yellow feet, most of his toenails were gone and what remained lay gnarled and grey and dying.

Dead John said he used to hitchhike to Frisco in three hours, but now nobody seemed to stop anymore, at least not for him. The kid was different, he could cop a ride pretty quick but he'd made a promise and now he was learning that that wasn't always the best thing to do. The kid had a name but he didn't like to use it. Bevan, who was called Bevan? When he was eight years old, one of his mom's boyfriends had put a bullet in an old Colt .45, stuck the barrel to the kid's head, pulled down his Wranglers and made Bevan open his mouth and suck on his penis. When the man came, he pulled the trigger and it was just a click, but from then on Bevan kept hearing that sound, click click click. Bad things happened to Bevan, bad things that other kids wouldn't even comprehend. Why he didn't know, but after a while a certain type of man could just smell Bevan coming, even if they couldn't quite see him yet they'd put their heads back on their shoulders and start sniffing the air. Bevan, Bevan, click click click.

The next day was different somehow. The sun came out, gentle like, and they caught a ride with an old black man who kept talking about Jesus and he took them all the way to the Bay Bridge on-ramp and let them off and gave Bevan five dollars and said, 'Boy, what are you doin' with this old serpent? Hey son, can't you tell?' And Bevan had shrugged his shoulders and grabbed his duffel bag and followed after Dead John who was making his way down the ice plants to Mission Street like it was the first day of summer vacation.

'SAN FRAN SAN FRAN SAN FRANCISCO, SAN FRAN SAN FRAN SAN FRANCISCO, OH YEAH.' When Bevan caught up to Dead John that's what he was singing and his old brown eyes were glimmering with years of memories, most of them bad, but there had been a couple… 'Ok, so there's two places you need to know right here. Two blocks up is Mission and 16th and three quarter of a mile up Mission is Polk Street, and that is were you make your money, and 16th and Mission is where we spend it,' and Dead John opened up his bottle of dihydrocodeine tablets and gave Bevan his issue of three and swallowed six for himself. 'Now kid, we're goin' to Polk Street first and then we are gonna get some proper fuckin' drugs. My god, yes we are.'

And don't you know it; for once it was just like Dead John said. In forty minutes Bevan had made a hundred and twenty dollars and in sixty minutes they were back on 16th and Mission and Dead John's sallow cheeks were fat and pink from all the balloons he had stuck in between his gums and the few stumps he had left of his teeth.

After three days they realised they had a pretty good routine and Dead John even said they could afford a room in a Hindu crack hotel, they just had to have a little discipline and not spend every penny on crack and chiva. So they did and that's when the dreams started to happen.

Bevan hadn't slept in a bed for a long time; he slept outside like all runaways are supposed to and the crazy thing was now that he was safe and warm, the insides of his head decided to open up and explode all over the motel room walls.

Click.

And Bevan's eyes would open.

Click.

And he could feel the presence of something thick and dark and full of bad crouching next to his bed.

In Bevan's thoughts he had a gun under the pillow and lo he tried with all his strength to get his hand to reach under and grab it, but his hand wouldn't move. He could hear his breath coming in and out real fast but he was frozen. His body wasn't wired up to his mind anymore and the shadow thing stood up and he could see its shape on the curtains over the window and he was more frightened than he'd ever been in his life.

Click.

'J J J John,' Bevan managed to whisper, but it took all of the strength he could muster. 'JJJJJJJJohnnnnnn. PPPPllllleeeeaaaaassssseeee. Hhhheeeeelllllpppp. MMmmmeeeeee.' And then somehow he managed to get hold of the pillow with two shaking fingers and break the spell by tossing the pillow lamely at the shadow and fell out of his bed and then crawled out the motel door and lay in the light of the hallway, panting and spinning. He was safe in the hallway and in the light.

'What the fuck are you doin'?' said an angry Dead John, standing over Bevan's body in the hallway. And Bevan said, 'There's something in there, John, there's something in there comin' to get me.' And Dead John just snorted and spat on the carpet next to Bevan's hand and said, 'Get your ass back into the fuckin' bed and stop with this bullshit.' And Bevan had stood up slowly and gone back into the room, but from that moment on he refused to turn out the light. 'No darkness, yeah?' he said to Dead John, who shook his head and wrapped a dirty T-shirt around it to cover his eyes. 'Crazy fuckin' fool,' said Dead John and he fell back to sleep.

The next afternoon at about three, Bevan got picked up by a lady with red hair who came down Polk Street in her white Mercedes. He'd thought he must have been dreaming again. 'Hi,' she'd said. 'Hi,' he replied. She was pretty and a little drunk. She must have been about forty and she had these green eyes that flashed like emeralds and beautiful white skin that looked soft and expensive.

'Listen,' she said, 'I need someone to help me go grocery shopping, I'm a little drunk,' and she laughed, then looked at him and smiled. 'Do you think you could help me pick up some stuff and carry it up to my apartment?' 'Yeah,' he said, 'I sure can.' But she'd taken him to this expensive restaurant in North Beach instead of the store and put them in a booth with candles and said hello to the waiter and ordered them lobster and spaghetti and ice cream, then she'd kicked off her shoes under the table and started rubbing her stockinged feet up and down Bevan's leg under the table while she drank white wine and waved at some people she knew at the other end of the restaurant. When they got back to her Mercedes she'd pushed him up against the passenger door and stuck her hands down his jeans and grabbed his cock real hard and squeezed it tight, staring him all crazy in the eyes going, 'What's this? Huh?' And squeezing it again and then saying, 'What's this little thing in my hands, huh? Is that your little cock, kid? Huh? Is that all you got?' Then she'd bitten him on the neck and laughed when he'd pulled her back by the hair because she'd hurt him. When they got in the car his hands were shaking because he wanted to fuck her so much but she wouldn't let him.

After they got to her apartment she took off her panties and her stockings and sat up on the kitchen counter by the microwave and made him lick her pussy while she rubbed her clitoris real fast with the fingers of her right hand. He could see the big diamond ring she had on going round and round before his eyes like a spinning top in front of the soft red hair. When she'd come, she started crying a bit and pushed him back and put on her panties and stockings and reached in her purse and gave him sixty dollars and walked down to the car and drove him back to Polk Street in silence. Boy, would I like to rob her, Bevan thought as they drove through the night streets. He thought about how she'd bitten his neck and laughed at him when he'd pulled her hair and then he started hearing the goddamned clicks from someplace deep inside his head.

Click.

Click.

Click.

The Parolees

Today was the day he was up earlier than usual, which was pretty early. The rest of the wing was still asleep and grey state issue blankets were lying on the floor around the legs of the bunks or piled like dead flowers on the tops of lockers. He opened the yellow envelope again, which had his parole conditions folded inside and knew he was going to run. He'd had a sergeant's UA eight days ago and he'd been dirty so he'd cut an empty tube of Colgate in half, melted the open end tight with a lighter and attached a shoelace with two safety pins through it, one for the tube and the other for the band on the inside of his boxers, then he hung it down by his dick and practiced flipping the cap open and shut with his right thumb, and when he thought he had it down pretty good, he got Rocky to piss clean and fill it up. After they called his number his heart had been bouncing out of his rib cage, but the sergeant hadn't even bothered to go into the cubicle like he was supposed to; he just stood outside the door looking bored.

At six am he popped his locker and dragged the water bag he'd made out of trashliners stuck inside a cotton mesh laundry sack for doing curls into the shower room and stabbed it with the end of a mop handle. The water glugged out and flowed down the drain in the middle of the floor. He stepped out of his boxers and pressed the cold beneath his favorite showerhead, the one closest to the window that just caught a view of the desert past the walls from the last mirror on the sink line. As he stood in the stream he placed his arms above his head and turned his back to the mirror to get a last look at the tattoos he'd picked up this term. Not bad, he thought, they'd made some good ink and Brandon got better each time he came back, which was just fine because Brandon wasn't going anywhere soon.

When he got back to his bunk Perry was sprawled across his mattress and Rocky was sitting on the end. They both had fat smiles on their faces. He motioned Perry to sit up so he could put on his socks and sat down next to them.

'Today's the day, dog,' said Perry. He nodded his head. 'What you gonna do?' He lit a roll-up and handed the lighter to Rocky and said, 'Keep it youngster.' Then he pointed to his locker and said, 'All that shit's for you two, ok? There's half a can of Bugler, two bags of coffee, a case of soups and some *Hustlers*. You guys take care, all right? Give some to Topo and Mel and give the handballs to Puppet in 302.' 'Ok,' said Rocky. 'Thanks man,' said Perry. 'But what you gonna do?' 'I'm gonna run like always, what the fuck else am I gonna do?' 'Stay down, dog' said Rocky. 'Stay down, dog,' said Perry and started going through the locker.

He didn't have any dress outs, he never did. The cops would point him to a cupboard full of abandoned jeans and sneakers and T-shirts and jackets and he would try his luck. He'd hoped they'd let him take his state issue boots – they fitted him perfectly and he'd worn them for sixteen months now. He did everything in them: play handball, do pull-ups, he even played peaknuckle in them and they weighted him good for leg lifts. He'd got a pair of long, red boxers' laces from Topo and doubled them around the tops of the boots when he tied them. With his cut-off black sweats and his extra-large white T-shirt he felt just right. On the street clothes were just a camouflage; he gauged what he wore by what he needed to do. In prison he could relax a little and figure out who he really was, but when the gates opened up all that was over.

At seven o'clock he was in the parole pen waiting for transport up to the hill and his 200 dollars. There were five other men paroling, all Chicanos, none of them going north. They were laughing and joking in Spanish, some had been down a while, they were quieter – it was the short-timers who made most of the noise, like kids at Christmas. They'd be back soon enough, just like him.

There was a van waiting outside the gates to take them to Norco where he would catch the bus to Ontario airport and pay 49 dollars for his PSA ticket to Oakland, then jump on Bart and head under the bay, breathing deeply until the doors opened at 16th and Mission. She was going to be happy to see him – she always was for a couple of days until it got crazy again.

When they got in the van there was a blonde girl at the back – he guessed she was paroling from the women's prison on the hill. She was pretty but looked dope sick;

she was sneezing in threes and rocking back and forward in her seat. The men stared at her like hungry dogs and the cop said, 'No talking 'till Norco or you're violated, mother-fuckers,' and they laughed and lit up their Marlboro's and rolled down the window and one guy said, 'Hey officer, put on some tunes man, let's hear some fuckin' music for La Raza,' and they all cheered.

Everyone had someone to meet them at Norco, except for him and the girl. As the prison van drove away she walked over to him and said, 'Hey, are you going to the airport?' He nodded his head and she said, 'Come on, let's share a cab.' She had milk white skin and her hair was dyed dry yellow and there was way too much mascara on her eyes, and he felt nervous because it had been a while. 'How come you're dope sick?' he said.

'Shit, I turned myself in five days ago 'cos I knew I had a release date coming and if it passed while I was out I'd do a twelve-month violation.'

'Didn't you take something with you?'

'Yeah, but it didn't hold me. It's no big deal, I got something waiting for me in Oakland.'

They caught a yellow cab out front and sat in the back seat quietly looking out at the suburban desert going by. At Ontario he handed the cabbie a twenty and said, 'Keep the change.' After they bought their tickets and he was in front of her heading to the gate she started to laugh and he turned around and said, 'What's funny?' 'Nothing,' she said. 'Just thinking.'

They sat together on the plane, her by the window. She pressed her face against the glass, looking out as they took off and as they got to the clouds he could see she was look-ing at him in the reflection. 'Want a drink?' he said. 'Sure.' 'Brandy ok?' 'Yeah.'

He bought four miniature Korbels and poured the brandy into the two plastic cups filled with ice, then set hers on the tray in front of her. He kept his hand on her drink for longer than he ought to. She reached out her right hand and took the drink from his fingers and then put her left hand into his and squeezed it hard, then leaned over and lay her head on his shoulder.

'You got a girl?'

'Yeah.'

'Is she pretty?'

'Yeah.'

'Are you gonna see her today?'

'If I can find her.'

'Don't you know were she lives?'

'Ah, she'll be in a hotel somewhere in the Mission. Everyone knows her down there; I just got to ask around.'

'Is she a hooker?'

'Yeah.'

She was quiet for a while, then reached up her other hand and opened his fingers and started drawing invisible hearts inside his palm with the edge of a broken fingernail.

'You know, I used to trick, but then I met Bob and he's been looking after me for five years now. He's a good guy but sometimes I get so bored I just wanna go crazy.'

'What's he do?' he said, pretending to be interested.

'Oh, he owns a little family plumbing business. He got me on methadone and put me in college and bought me a cat and pays all the bills, but I've put on so much weight and I just sit around watching TV and I'm bored out of my head. So I started dipping again and picked up two dirties and was gonna get violated, so Bob arranged for me to come down and turn myself in.'

They were quiet again, then she put her lips to his ear and whispered, 'Do you want to fuck me in the toilet?' 'Sure,' he said. 'You go down first then I'll follow in a minute.' 'Ok,' he said and finished his drink, put the tray into its place in the seat in front of him and walked down the aisle to the back of the plane.

The Hitchhiker

He'd been squatting on his haunches for over an hour with his leather jacket draped backwards over his shoulders like a blanket. His neck hurt from holding his head to the right as he searched for any sign of headlights coming down the hill from Buellton. He'd made a big mistake getting off Highway Five with the last ride – the man had talked him into coming to Solvang for pancakes at Denny's and he'd been hungry so he just said ok. Now he was stuck thirty miles from a highway and the man had gone to work, but he'd given him ten dollars and bought him a pack of Camel straights before dropping him off on this piece of shit road saying, 'Son, you'll catch a ride from here straight down to Carpintaria and then it's just ninety miles down the coast to LA – you should be there by morning.' He'd been a good guy, he just wanted someone to talk to, but he didn't know shit about hitchhiking.

Crows were fighting in the trees behind him and every now and then one would swoop out chased by two others. He took a harmonica out of the back pocket of his black Dickies and tried to play something to warm him up but it just drained him. He put the harmonica back in his pocket and stood up to stretch his legs, then reached down and grabbed a handful of rocks from the dust and started throwing them at the sign across the road. He aimed for the 'o' in the middle of Solvang and said to himself, 'Now if I hit that 'o' in Solvang a ride's gonna appear and take me straight to Hollywood, and if I don't that means I gotta cross the road and go north to San Francisco.' He took aim and fired and hit it dead center.

Hollywood was shit. The sun was long gone and now it was just dope fiends and winos and fucked up whores, all of them hunting for money, just like him. He had a number for some guy who made porn films written on the back of a business card that he'd been given by a ride in San Luis Obispo: 'Kid, with a cock like yours you'll make a fortune, I guarantee it!'

He was dirty, his socks were glued to his feet and he could smell his own sweat through his jacket. 'I need a fuckin' shower. I need a fuckin' shower and some clean clothes before I'm calling anyone.'

At two am on La Cienega he came across a blue sleeping bag rolled up underneath a dumpster. He bent down and pulled it out, it smelled like piss but he was cold and tired, he just wanted to sleep and he thought that in the morning he'd know what to do. He picked up a flat of cardboard and walked down a small alley at the side of a Wells Fargo bank. At the back it opened out into a small empty parking lot and there were some shrubs over by a chain link fence. He walked over, looked around and thought, this will do. He dropped the cardboard and took off his boots, lay down and pulled the sleeping bag over him loose, then he opened his buck knife and fell asleep holding it tight in his right hand.

At seven am he woke up to somebody kicking his legs through the sleeping bag. When he opened his eyes he saw a tall Mexican security guard standing over him.

'Come on fella, you need to move.'

'What the fuck, you didn't have to kick me man.'

'You got two minutes, pick up your shit and go.'

He sat up and put on his boots and folded the blade back into place, then stood and walked down the alley leaving the sleeping bag where it lay.

At ten am he came through the doors of a St. Vincent de Paul charity store on La Brea. He picked up a pair of socks, a white T-shirt and a 30 by 34 pair of blue Levi's, stuck them under his jacket and walked out the front door. He crossed the road and went into McDonald's, headed straight into the men's at the back and took off all his clothes. He stuck his feet into the blue water of the toilet and flushed it three times, then stood at the sink and gave himself a birdbath using his old T-shirt as a towel. When he was done he put on his new clothes and combed his hair back with his fingers and looked in the mirror. 'That's better man,' he said and winked at his reflection, then he stuck his old clothes in the trashcan and walked out the door.

Hollywood looked better in the morning; blonde girls and BMWs and Porsches and palm trees and money, he could smell the money. He felt good and hungry at the same time. He picked up half a cigarette from the sidewalk and lit it with his Zippo, leaned against a lamp post and took out his harmonica from the back pocket of his new jeans with his right hand and held it up to his mouth and played the first part of 'Midnight Rambler' by The Stones while he stuck his left hand out with his thumb in the air and waited for a ride.

Ten minutes later he was in the front seat of a Chrysler Cordoba with an old man sporting a shaved head and a well-trimmed white goatee. He was thin and smelt like women's perfume and was tapping his finger tips on the steering wheel in time to Nat King Cole singing, 'There was a boy, a strange enchanted boy.'

'Are you hungry?' said the old man, looking in the rear-view mirror.

'Kinda,' said the boy.

'How about some huevos rancheros at my house and a pot of strong coffee? I mean, if you have the time.' The boy shrugged his shoulders. 'Where are you headed to anyway?'

'Hollywood,' said the boy.

'Well,' the old man said after a while, 'I guess you've arrived.'

He lived on the second floor of a white Hacienda stucco apartment block. He opened the door and stood back smiling and made a little roll in the air with his right hand like he was a courtier at some faggot palace welcoming the returning prince. 'After you sir,' he said. The boy stepped inside and walked over the cream shagpile carpet to a leather sofa and sat down.

'Ok if I smoke?' said the boy.

'Of course, of course,' said the old man, 'I'll just get you an ashtray.'

He went into the kitchen and returned with an abalone shell and a can of Budweiser. 'Here's a refreshment,' he said with a wink, then stood and watched the boy as he lit a cigarette and placed it in the abalone shell on the coffee table in front of him and sat back into the leather sofa with the beer in his hand.

'Well, you're a handsome fellow aren't you,' said the old man. The boy shrugged his shoulders again. 'So how old are you, fifteen? Sixteen?'

'I'm eighteen next week,' said the boy.

'Oh my, congratulations,' said the old man then stood there looking down at him with a fake smile on his old faggot face.

It was the same as it usually was; after he'd made break-fast the old man put on a porno of a white lady getting fucked by two black guys, the boy undid the buttons on his jeans and the old man knelt over him and whispered some stupid shit to his cock then sucked it like it was the straw on a thick vanilla milkshake, while the boy sat and watched the expression on the woman's face as the black fuckers humped her in the ass and the pussy at the same time. He liked to look at her eyes on the screen, he could tell if she was real or not by her eyes, all the rest of it was just bullshit. When he came the old man lay his head on the boys knees long enough to make him feel uneasy. 'Ok,' said the boy, 'I need to piss.'

In the bathroom he went through the cabinets and drawers and pocketed a bottle of Percocet and some cufflinks. When he came out there was forty dollars on the table and the old man was standing at the door with his car keys in his hand.

'Can I drop you anywhere?' he said.

'Yeah,' said the boy, 'back where you found me.' And just for a second he thought about getting his buck knife out and taking the old faggot's car and his wallet, but the old man already had the door open and a lady was walking up the corridor to her apartment across the hall.

'Hi there, Bud,' she said to the old man.

'Hi Gladys,' he replied.

When they got in the car the old man handed him a business card and said, 'Here's my number kid, if you're stuck give me a call.' Then he was quiet. When they pulled up to the McDonald's on La Brea the old man put his hand on the boy's arm and said, 'You know, you look just like my nephew, what a handsome young man.'

'Yeah,' said the boy, 'I bet he is,' and he stepped out onto the sidewalk and walked on up the street leaving the car door open behind him.

The Fish

He thought it was like a tuna boat and that they were the tuna, flapping around on the wet deck, naked and squeezing their way into the showers. There had to be a hundred men at a time coming down the tier and onto the metal steps, clutching white towels around their waistlines and pushing their way down into line for the water. It felt wrong, so many men pushing up against you, laughing and swearing and calling out to their friends or watching their backs for enemies, but you couldn't do nothing about it but go with the tide.

The whites broke off and headed into the concrete pen on the right, pushing and shoving their way to get underneath one of the six showerheads that shot out a lukewarm spray from the old pipes that ran along the thick walls of the block. The blacks all went down to the pen on the left and the Mexicans and Indians filled the space that was left in between. Some men had their boxers and their socks in their hands and were trying to wash them with white bars of state issue soap at the same time as they were washing themselves. They had to be quick because they had seven minutes from the time they unlocked the gates on the tier to the time you had to be back in the cell.

He didn't make it. He hadn't fought hard enough to get to the water, he had just stood back and expected someone to let him in, but nobody had and when the sergeant called over the intercom, 'Lock 'em up. Third tier, that's it, that's all. Back to your cells,' he'd been pushed out of the way and he'd slipped and landed on his knees and got crushed by the tide of naked prisoners heading back to the stairs and when he'd managed to stand up again and had finally stuck his head under a jet of water the fourth tier was on its way down to the showers and he found himself smashed up against the side of the railings as he struggled through the crush to get back to his cell.

It was locked, they were all locked. 'Third tier secure,' said the intercom and he found himself standing alone on the walkway bare-assed except for the white towel that was too small to go all the way round his waist, so he had to hold it with his hand pressed on his stomach in order to cover his penis.

He leaned over the side of the railings and tried to catch the attention of the sergeant at the desk all the way down by the big wooden doors at the front of the block, but the sergeant ignored him, so then he waved up at the gunner on the fifth tier catwalk that ringed the exterior wall and shouted.

'Excuse me, hello!'

'What?' said the gunner.

'I'm locked out,' he said.

'Too bad,' said the gunner, 'stand by your cell and wait.'

'For how long?' he said, but the gunner had already gone.

He walked up to the gate of his cell and stood close to it so that the other prisoners along the tier would stop watching him from behind the flaked metal bars that ran the full length of the walkway. His cellmate was standing in the back of the small cell trying to shave in the steel mirror that was bolted to the wall above the metal sink and to the left of the toilet bowl. He had been in the cell for two days and the only thing the man had said to him was, 'Do you got any tobacco?' And when he had said, 'No, I don't have anything,' that had been the end of all conversation.

It was cold and he was naked and he felt stupid and exposed and for the life of him he couldn't see how he was going to cope with this nightmare, and he thought how it must have been for the people at Treblinka, stripped bare and herded into the showers with the gunners all around them, and part of him wished that he could have been gassed too, instead of having to stand there dumb and wet and naked and scared. Fuck this, he thought, fuck this.

The next time they ran showers he didn't wait around, he was first out of the cell and down the tier and pushing his way to the front of the crowd of naked prisoners and when he got under the showerhead he took his sweet time washing his ass and his feet and his hair and when some guy tried to push him out of the way he planted his bare feet and stood firm and then he dropped his bar of soap into one of the socks that he was going to wash and he spun it around till the soap sat at the bottom of the sock and slung it over his shoulder so that everyone could see. He finished rinsing off and walked back up to his cell with his cellmate behind him, and after they'd bolted the tier and he'd put on his new jumpsuit his cellmate reached out his hand and said, 'Hey kid, my name's Dago, where are you from?' And he'd said, 'San Francisco,' and Dago had said, 'Nice town, shame about the faggots,' and he'd smiled and then said, 'Well, they got to live somewhere,' and Dago had laughed and patted him on his shoulder and said, 'Do you want a smoke,' and he'd said yeah sure. After Dago had rolled them a couple smokes and handed him one and then lit it for him and they were sitting on Dago's bunk with their backs against the cell wall, he felt himself relaxing from someplace deep inside. Fuck, he thought, this ain't so bad after all.

The Rope Swing

There were three of them; they were about twelve or thirteen. They cut down the trail of the ravine like bucks coming down a mountain. They moved fast because that's how they'd done it since they could remember. Tommy was at the back. He had a paper Safeway bag held tight in his arms and every time his feet hit a rock or a branch you could hear the bottles inside clink together. Dickie Donnelly was upfront with his dumb smile and his blonde hair poking out of the black beanie he always wore, a carton of Tarrlytons in his left hand. They didn't know if they were being followed and every now and then they'd stop to listen, but as they got further into the ravine they started to relax.

'Nobody saw us man, I'm tellin' you.'

'Well, two cars came down Lexington as we were climbing over the fence.'

'But they didn't fuckin' stop, did they? I'm tellin' you they didn't see us.'

'We're gonna get drunk, we're gonna get drunk, we're gonna get motherfuckin' wasted,' sang Paul in the middle, and reached over to open the top of the bag in Tommy's arms.

'Just look at that liquor, I'm gonna puke all night.'

'Come on dickhead,' said Tommy, 'let's see if she's still there.'

She was sitting outside the old plywood fort just up the hill from the rope swing. She didn't have any shoes on and her brown hair was full of twigs and dead leaves. She was trying to get her Zippo to catch light one more time so she could smoke the last bit of a roach she had wrapped in a matchbook cover. Her thumb was blistered from striking the roller on the Zippo again and again.

'Hey,' said Tommy.

'Hey,' said the girl.

'We got some liquor and cigarettes and some bags of beef jerky,' said Tommy, lifting up the bag in his arms.

'You got a light?' said the girl.

'I do,' said Dickie.

'Well come on up here, what you waitin' for?' she replied and patted the dirt at her side.

Maybe she was fourteen, maybe she was eighteen, you couldn't tell. She'd run away a week ago and had been sleeping nights in the fort down the ravine. In the mornings she would climb up and wait at the school bus stop and the kids would give her sandwiches out of the bag lunches that their mothers had made for them. Her stepfather had been looking for her each evening at six when he got home from work. He walked around the neighborhood offering the kids twenty bucks if they told him where she was hiding – so far no-one had said but it was just a matter of time.

They started with a fifth of Southern Comfort and chain-smoked the Tarrlytons and when she went to open the Bell's Tommy said, 'Hey let's play spin the bottle,' because he was feeling brave with the alcohol and she was bored so she said, 'Ok' and they sat in a circle and span the empty Southern Comfort bottle and whatever boy it landed on went into the fort with her holding his hand for the length of time it took to smoke a cigarette, then the other two would start throwing rocks at the plywood walls and shouting, 'Come on motherfucker, time's up let's spin again.'

Two days later she was gone. They couldn't figure out what happened because her jacket and her shoes were still inside the fort. Some kids said she must have fallen off the rope swing, which span over the ravine almost sixty feet high, but nobody liked to go all the way down the cliff to check because it was hard to climb back up again.

The Manta Ray

I was spearfishing in Baja. I was drunk most of the time and we lived in this old van I bought in San Diego, just driving down dirt roads, me and this crazy bitch from Seattle. She had the whitest skin and jet-black hair and she wore a straw cowboy hat and big, mirrored shades. We had a fat box of pills because the whole idea of being there was to run away from the heroin. See what I mean? Stupid and drunk. Imagine going to Mexico to kick a habit.

Ah fuck it – one afternoon I'd shot a couple reef fish and it was getting dark so I was trying to cook 'em quick but I couldn't get the logs to catch, so I poured some gasoline from a jerrycan over the pit and struck a match. And wouldn't you know, the wind comes in off the sea and drags the spark to the top of the gas can and the whole thing goes up. Like a dumb shit I kick it over because I think it's gonna explode and the flames jump out with the gas and wrap around my legs and I'm fucking on fire. I mean, both of my legs are burning like a forest fire and I yell my head off and try to run into the water but I trip and I'm rolling in the sand with the stink of my swimming trunks melting into the skin of my legs. Anyway, some fat Mexican guy who'd been sitting with his family watching the sun go down comes running over with a blanket and smothers it over my legs and his wife shows up with a bucket of sea water and throws it on top of the blanket, which is on top of my legs and my skin opens up and swallows the fibers which I didn't know until they tried to take it off me later and I screamed because the whole thing had melted into my flesh. But that's not the point. I don't even know what the point is except that they dragged me up the beach and propped me against the trunk of a palm tree and he hands me a bottle of Kahlua and as I'm drinking it I can see the sun's going down, dropping like a red saucer into the sea of Cortez and I have a few more hits on the Kahlua and I'm starting to feel different, kind of quiet and still and that's when I see it.

It was a giant manta ray. It came flying up out of the sea straight into the middle of the sun and it seemed to go up forever, then it twisted in mid air and did a complete summersault and landed smooth as a knife blade and disappeared.

I passed out drunk and when I woke up I was shaking all over. It was the craziest thing; I wasn't in pain but my whole body was jerking and twitching like a vibrator. Later I figured I'd gone into shock but at the time you don't know that you're in another world, but I kept seeing that manta ray break water and head up into the sun and spin a circle, just for the fuck of it, you know. It's one of the best things I've ever seen and the funny thing is I had to set myself on fire just to notice it.

So about the girl. I get them mixed up sometimes, but

this time I know who I'm talking about – that crazy bitch in the cowboy hat and shades. Three months in Mexico and all she ever wore was this black bikini and spangled six-inch stilettos, stumbling down the beach with a bottle of mescal in one hand and a fucking Gudang Garam clove cigarette in the other like she's on the catwalk in Milan. 'Honey, I want to fuck,' she'd say and I'd say, 'Ok darling,' and she'd drop to her knees right on the beach and we'd fuck and I'd knock her cowboy hat off and stick her face in the sand because that's how she liked it, and then we'd go for a swim and fuck some more in the water, and when we came out she'd put on some lipstick and dust the sand off her cowboy hat and stick it back on her head.

Her name? You don't need to know her name, it doesn't fucking matter, ok?

Fuck it. Well the next morning I'm still sitting up on the palm tree and a pickup truck comes down the dust track and it's the fat Mexican – his wife has sent him to check on me and he can see the blanket is melted to my legs so he starts pointing to his truck and saying, 'Medico, medico' and I say, 'Si, medico,' and him and the crazy bitch who's woken up at this point help me to my feet and drop me in the back of the pickup and they climb in front and we're off to the medico.

All I remember is desert and a white concrete shed with a red cross painted on top of the front door and inside are these young Mexican girls in white dresses who point to a metal table and I climb on top and they try to take the blanket off and I start yelling, 'Motherfuckers, mother-fuckers!' so they strap me down to the table and get scissors and tongs and shiny surgical blades and one of them picks up a big bottle of iodine and pours it all over the blanket and my legs and they set to work ripping and cutting and scrubbing and peeling and the crazy bitch takes off her shades to get a better look and the fat Mexican walks backwards slowly out the door and I'm trying to get the manta ray to rise up out of the water, but he's long gone and it's just me. It's just me and the angels who smile with compassion as I'm screaming, 'Where's the drugs, you useless fuckin' Mexican whores? You cunt suckin' bitches, where's the fuckin' morphine?'

So, where was I? Oh yeah, after our little session, that fat Mexican, bless his heart, drives us back to his hovel with scrawny chickens and little pigs running round the yard and his wife insists on cooking us carnitas and frijoles and he gets out two big bottles of Kahlua and we proceed to get drunk and his fat babies are playing in the dust with the chickens and crazy bitch picks up two piglets and starts kissing their little snouts and walking around the table, wiggling her ass and singing to the piggies. I can see the fat Mexican's in love with her; his eyes are glued to her black bikini bottoms as she parades around the table doing her thing and then he jumps up and goes over to where his wife is slapping tortillas and scoops her into his arms and waddles back to where I'm sitting and drops her in my lap with a big smile on his face like he's just remembered the story of Lot and his daughters.

Up close she is pretty and young and smells like warm milk and I can tell that she's embarrassed but she's staring into my big blue eyes and I reach up a hand and brush the hair out of her Indian face. Just for a second I felt connected to something good, kind of like the manta ray, or the feeling you get when all the charges have been dropped and you think, just maybe, it's all gonna be different. But then crazy bitch starts squealing like the piglets, 'Naughty, naughty, naughty,' she's singing and the fat Mexican is crashing into chairs, trying to catch her and the babies are crying and I come back to life and put down his wife and rise out of my chair and grab a big metal skillet off the table and hold it up in the air and bring it down gently on the back of his head.

I know, you're thinking that doesn't make sense – bring it down gently on the back of his head – what's he fucking talking about? But hey, believe me or not, sometimes gentle violence is the best way to illustrate the big picture.

The next morning the fat Mexican shows up at our spot on the beach by the van. He shows up with his hat in his hand, all humble and meek and begs our forgiveness and says how he doesn't remember anything but his wife told him he must come and apologize and he's so sorry. He doesn't look at crazy bitch, not once, and he hands me a bag full of carnitas and frijoles and corn tortillas, then jumps back in his pickup and drives away.

So now it's just me and crazy bitch at the bottom of Baja and it's fucking hot and I'm not supposed to go in the water and I think, fuck it, and start duct-taping plastic bags round my leg, taking my spear gun and heading out in the morning. When I come back crazy bitch has all these Vitamin E gel capsules and she takes a pin and pops them and gently rubs the fluid into my burns and she takes off her hat and her shades so she can see what she's doing and for a whole month she does this every day and you know what, those burns all healed up pink and perfect. I think we even kissed a couple of times instead of just fuck and when we drove back over the border we realized we'd had a pretty good time.

Oh yeah, her name was Prudence. Prudence Maryanne McLintock. She didn't mean any harm. Like I said, she was just a crazy bitch.

The Escort

She couldn't tell you why she started tricking, it just seemed to happen. She thought most of the things in her life had been the same way, like she was a tumbleweed being blown across America without any say in the matter. If you pressed her she would say, 'Well I suppose I was sitting in a doorway on Market and 8th early one morning. I think it was raining and I went to a phone booth to call my mother to tell her I was safe and I saw a card stuck up by the coin slot that said "Escorts required, no experience necessary, top dollar paid," so I called the number instead of my mother and this girl by the name of Jackie answered and she seemed real nice. She gave me her address and said she'd pay the cab fare if I went right away, so I jumped in a taxi and that's how it started.'

Her first job had been at the Hyatt Regency in Burlingame at twelve o'clock that same day. Jackie had given her her own pager and introduced her to Jerry who was going to be her driver and told her how it worked. 'When you get in the room, honey, the first thing you do is make sure you feel safe, then get the cash up front and call me to say time's started and make sure I've got the right room number, then in forty minutes I'll call you back to say time's up and if he wants to spend more money we'll go in thirty minute slots at a hundred each from there – got it?' She'd nodded her head and said 'I think so.'

The first guy had been Japanese. It had been easy – he was small and came fast and smelled clean and when she left the room with 250 dollars, two thirds of it hers, she felt the best she had in a long time.

On the fourth day of working she'd gone to a job in a small motel in North Beach and Jerry had dropped her off and taken another girl, Amanda, to a call in China Town, so she was alone. When she got to the room a big Mexican guy opened the door and she could see two other guys sitting on the couch drinking vodka. Something had told her no, don't go in there, but she did. That was the first time she'd done heroin and she'd got so sick and could barely remember anything that happened except that the next day she was sore, but they'd paid her so she guessed it was alright.

After two weeks of staying at Jackie's she got her own room at the Hotel Utah on Harrison and 3rd. It was a 120 dollars a week and she had to share the toilet and the kitchen, but there was a bar in the basement where all the bike messengers and motorcycle couriers hung out and on Friday night they had bands and an old Vietnamese lady made the best food on a little gas ring stove they had in the back. Everyone knew her name and she could even run up a tab at the bar and put it on her room bill. She had just turned eighteen but nobody carded her and she felt like she was truly grown up.

After a month she had saved 2,000 dollars, so she bought a ticket for her mom to fly out from Dallas, but when her mom got there she hadn't believed she was just having dinner and going to the theatre with rich business-men, like she told her when she came home at six o'clock in the morning on the Sunday. They were meant to go to Golden Gate Park but her mom had gotten off the couch and slapped her and called her a whore and pulled her hair, so she'd run out of the hotel and gone to a bar on Bryant and 4th and cried as she drank shots of tequila with beer backs. When she got back to the room later that night her mother had left. She didn't see her again for a long time after that.

She met Gary Wayne sitting on the staircase in the hotel playing an old acoustic guitar. She was on her way up to her room after finishing work and he was singing 'Pale Blue Eyes' by the Velvet Underground and she thought that she'd never heard anything so perfect before. She had looked at him and smiled, but he just kept singing and when he was done she'd said, 'Do you want to come up?'

She stopped taking speed because Jackie had said she was already too thin and started snorting coke instead. Jerry always had coke because sometimes the clients wanted to buy some. They'd say to her, 'Do you want to party?' And she'd say 'Yeah', and they'd say, 'Can you get any coke?' and she'd say 'Yeah', and they'd give her the money and she'd page Jerry who was parked up outside. It was as easy as that at first.

After three months things got strange. She couldn't say why except that sometimes Jerry frightened her because he kept a pistol under the driver's seat and he'd stare in the rear-view mirror real hard then reach down for the pistol and when she said, 'What's wrong?' he wouldn't answer, he just kept staring. And Jackie started talking about weird clicks on the phone and told her not to use certain words when she called from the guys' hotel rooms, but she kept forgetting and Jackie got mad and called her stupid and sometimes Jerry wouldn't be in the parking lot when she came out like he was supposed to be and she'd be left standing outside and it felt like everyone could tell what she'd been doing.

So then one day she just took off instead of waiting for him and she spent the money on coke and didn't pay Jackie her third and the next day she moved to a hotel in the Tenderloin so they couldn't find her and that night she went out on the street for the first time.

The Broken Nazi

Kitten was an ugly bitch. She was tall and bony with big feet and long spatula fingers, she had hard, black silicone tits on her chest and a huge dick that she strapped up between her ass cheeks before she put on her panties. Kitten would take a hit of crack and lick her lips and whisper, 'I'm rather partial to white cock, you know,' and smile as she handed me her straight shooter. 'Well,' I'd say, 'for five bucks you can suck mine,' and she'd laugh and pat me on the head then put on her old fur and head out to work. In those days it was so simple: I'm a rat and you're a dog and we hunt through the garbage pile of a world that we live in, there's no need for excuses and time dissolves into the space between one shot and the next.

Kitten had a boyfriend – Doo-wop Dave. They lived in the courtyard of an 18th Street community medical center in the Mission, by night that is. Every morning they'd have to roll up their blankets and cardboard and stash them in an old garage by Dolores Street before the people came to work. Doo-wop wasn't a criminal; he was a Vietnam vet who made little sculptures and wind chimes out of beercans and fishing line. Each morning when

Kitten went down to the Tenderloin to catch, Doo-wop would head up to Market and Castro and set out his stall on the pavement and sit on the ground playing his harmonica to his mongrel bitch pit bull. 'Hey Dave,' I said as I walked by him heading up to Twin Peaks to scout for open front windows on fag penthouse apartments or promising handbags left in between the front seats of Porsches or Mercedes. I had an old Everlast spark plug tied to a bit of string that, if you threw it just right, imploded the side windows of cars with a beautiful hushed crunch.

'Hey homeboy, got an outfit?' I turn around and there is this walking disaster staring at me with crazy speed eyes and a jaw that permanently rotates like the insides of a Rolex.

'What's it to you?' I inquire, very much doubting this guy has got anything to offer but a lot of police attention.

'My outfit's clogged man,' he whines, 'and I got a little taste of crank man, I'll do you the cotton.'

So this guy is a mess – he's got long, stringy blonde hair, ripped Levi's and a white T-shirt covered with bloodstains and bare filthy feet. But his crowning glory is the big, black tattoo that wraps around his neck like the Michelin name in lights on the blimp above the super bowl. 'CONTROLLED BY HATE' it says. Wow, I think. Wow.

Pigpen Mike got out of Quentin two days ago (for the seventeenth time) and has been running in circles around San Fran shooting the half ounce of meth he bought with his gate money and now there's only a wash to be had and he's as psychotic as a baboon wet nursed by a mop-head in some Cal Berkley lab.

'Yeah, I got an outfit,' I say, and fish out my backup from the inside of my left sock.

'Here man, don't worry about the cotton but when you're done how about making some cash?'

'Oh yeah man,' he says. 'I could use some fuckin' dollar.'

Then he pulls the plunger out of the barrel and rubs his last few flakes of cat piss from a now empty baggy straight into the chamber and takes a sip on his can of Schlitz, then squirts about 30cc of spit and beer inside. He covers it with his thumb and shakes it up like he's mixing a Mai Tai, then he pops the plunger back in, squeezes his fist tight a couple of times and jacks that spike into the crook of his left arm, throws back his head and starts barking kinda softly to the sky.

'Urrfff urrfff urrfff,' he says, then hands me back the outfit.

'Let's do it,' he says.

'Absolutely,' says I, putting the rocket back inside my sock.

'Abso-fuckin'-luutely…'

Some days are meant to be yours – I mean even pieces of shit can sometimes find that space where the god's smile down and whisper in your ear: Have at it boys. Well me and Pigpen don't make it a block before some executive faggot pulls up on the curb in his new silver Lexus and dives out of the car and runs into the post office on Castro, leaving the Lexus purring in front of our disbelieving eyes with the driver's door wide open like he was a valet at the Hilton.

'Wow,' I say.

'Oh wow.'

And we're gone. But the problem is Pigpen's first in the driver's seat and after burning the tires he stalls the car twice before the end of the block, takes a left, rear-ends some old lady in a Pinto, takes another left and we're back in front of the post office we started from. Now we were in a hurry.

'Get the fuck out of the seat,' I say. 'Get the fuck out, I'm driving you fuckin' moron,' and Pigpen just has this look like he knows something's going terribly wrong but he can't quite make out what it is. Anyway we swap seats, roll up the windows, lock the doors and I step on that plush Lexus accelerator...

Well, well, well, there's money in the Lexus. No shit, Pigpen flips open the glove compartment and there's an envelope full of twenties, '520, 540, 560, 600,' says Pigpen, and I'm kinda impressed that he can count that high. But what is definitely of the highest priority right now is turning that envelope full of dollar into some heroin and crack. What the fuck else are you gonna do with it? See what I mean – one minute you're slinking down Castro Street, dope sick and filthy, trying to make ten bucks and the next you're sporting a sweet ride with some cash.

As I pull up at the red light on Van Ness, heading to the TL to get Kitten I look over and see this fine redhead next to me behind the wheel of her Mazda RX7 and I put on the fag's sunglasses and look over at her and she smiles and I think, yeah man, I'm a happening dude now. And then she gets a spot on Pigpen and her smile turns into a look of horror and she's gone at the green like she's in the Indy

500 and I turn to Pigpen and say, 'Get in the back and lay down, man, you're gonna get us pulled over,' and he looks a little hurt and confused but he climbs over the seat anyway and lays down and falls a-fuckin'-sleep.

Every moment needs a master plan to snatch the most from its possibilities and my head's working overtime, but it's really quite simple. We get Kitten from the fire hydrant on Jones Street and drop her at the pay phone on Valencia with 200 for Puffy and Tuffy. Then I page Wello, the old Salvadorian, and he calls back real fast and I say, 'Una media ounce de negro por favor,' and in seven minutes he's at 15th and Shotwell. Then we park up in the underground car park of 17th and I even buy a parking ticket and we're into the liquor store and they get tequila and duct tape and crack pipes and Brillo and a carton of Camel straights and eight Bic lighters and we get a ten-bag of outfits from Hop-along Ned the one-legged old wino, and then we're up the piss-stinking stairs of the Mission Hotel and hand forty bucks to the Hindu on the desk and it's room number thirty four, all the way at the back on the top floor for two nights thank you very much, and hang on, we're not finished yet. I pull off all the sheets and blankets from the bed and duct tape them to the windows and set the desk up to barricade the front door and I think it's just about there. Yup. I set the little crowbar I carry tied to my left leg up on the door frame take one last look around and that's it, we're ready to descend...

Pigpen's from Modesto, but I don't really care, not one bit. As far as I'm concerned he's not meant to be here – his sole purpose was to run decoy, to go in first and pull all the heat so I could slide in and out like a ghost. Pigpen is a prime example of surplus requirements, kinda like Doo-wop Dave the Vietnam vet – now the war's over, for a moment, he's not needed or welcome. So Pigpen takes a big hit of crack and off comes the blood-stained T-shirt and bam, we get a shot on his immaculate torso, and it's just permeated in bad Nazi ink. He's sporting every white dickhead tattoo that's ever been dreamed of and then some. Lightning bolts, AB eagles, a hundred blue-black swastikas and on the middle of his stomach is a portrait of Adolf himself, in a full Nazi salute. Kitten's sitting on the bed getting her Brillo just right with her long black legs crossed like a school teacher and I can see her eyes running up and down Pigpen's graffiti and she makes a little sucking hiss with her teeth and tongue.

'Boy, what's this nasty piece of shit peckerwood doing here, huh?' She's getting warmed up now, and stands up on her four-inch red glitter stilettos with her feet planted like a sumo wrestler.

'What's this KKK motherfuckin' retarded republican doing on my side of the tracks?' Then she drops a boulder on the end of her straight shooter and sparks her pink Bic lighter and takes a forty dollar hit and holds it in while she stares all crazy eyed at Pigpen, who at this point looks about three years old. Then Kitten blows out her hit in Pigpen's face, runs her tongue around her lips and drops to her knees, gets a hold of Pigpen's belt and unbuckles it and he's frozen as she pops the buttons on his dirty Levi's one by one 'till they drop around his ankles and she reaches into his boxers and pulls out this huge white dick that's got stars and lightning bolts tattooed up and down it and she sighs with relief and pops the hole thing in her mouth and starts sucking the life up and out from his dumb white Nazi motherfucking toes.

So Kitten has been trained like a Pavlovian doggie from an early age to equate a hit of crack with a cock ramming down her esophagus; it's like strawberries and cream to her. But Pigpen's in new territory, now he's just a walking residue of a psychotic breakdown – he's a testament to the powers of crystal meth's ability to shed the illusion of humanity and leave just a husk in its place and somehow I kind of realized the sweetness of the incongruity I was witnessing in front of my eyes. A breaking down of cultural perceptions and belief systems; here was a white Nazi redneck from Modesto, he could have been Charlton Heston's grandson, being pinned to the wall by a six-foot-two black male transvestite with fake tits and wearing a spandex leotard, who's got her thumb up his asshole wriggling it about while she sucks down his white pride cock and both of his Nazi balls and he's helpless to do anything but roll his eyes and groan as he comes in spurts and rolls his jaw in dumb zombie circles.

'Amen,' I said. 'Amen brother, life's good when you're on the other side.'

The Whale

Purvis Johnson was old, he was older than he ever thought he was going to get to be and no matter what kind of pills he took or how many times the nurses changed the bandages on his ulcerated legs, he knew his day was coming.

In the evenings after dinner when they pushed him outside for a cigarette and a cup of black coffee, he liked to sit still beside a tree on the far end of the hospital parking lot and watch the people coming and going. They came in cars or got off buses at the bus stop down the way and walked on up to the automatic glass doors of the hospital entrance, pausing sometimes to take a last hit on their cigarettes before going inside, or they came in ambulances, flying up to the emergency entrance on the right of the building, rolled out on gurneys with tubes running up from their arms into plastic bags full of blood and saline and god knows what else. Gunshots, car wrecks, overdoses, attempted suicides, heart attacks, food poisoning, cerebral hemorrhages, stabbings, perforated bowels, kidney failure, advanced cirrhosis of the liver. My my, thought Purvis, there sure are a lot of ways for a man to die. And the thing was that no matter how long he sat out there he never saw the dead ones come back out. No, he thought, they sure don't come out this way, they must take 'em out by the back, there must be some alley that's locked up and private with CCTV cameras and high security so nobody can see, I guess they figure that people would get upset if they saw all those dead bodies, so they're trying to protect them and keep them happy. Purvis got another cigarette out from the pack in his pajama shirt pocket and put it between his thin lips and lit it with his lighter. He had to concentrate because his hand was shaking like a leaf in a spring wind, but he managed like he always did when he wanted something bad enough.

I love tobacco, thought Purvis as he blew the smoke out of his mouth in a velvet blanket that hung for a moment over his old head before drifting up to join the clouds making their way across the evening sky. I love tobacco and I love strong black coffee and I love a big girl with strong legs and crazy blue eyes and I love boxing and Hank Williams songs when they're sung right by someone with heart and I love the feeling you get when you're let out of jail and I love swimming in the ocean when you're a kid and the way it feels when a big wave crashes down on you and you're caught underneath getting tossed and turned and you don't know which way is up or down until you relax and just go with it and let it carry you along and the next thing you know is your head pops up and you take in a big breath of god's clean air, and Purvis smiled for a bit, then he took another hit on his cigarette and thought about the whale.

It was lying on the warm sand of the little beach just down from the cliffs on the other side of the Golden Gate

Bridge. It was about twenty foot long and its tail was flapping in the water, still trying to push itself further up the sand. It would stop for a bit and then it would start again like it had someplace really important it had to get to. They'd climbed down the cliff, him and his girl, and they'd walked up and down around the whale and he'd said, 'What the hell are you doin' Mr Whale?' And his girl had started crying and said, 'Purvis do something, he's tryin' to kill himself.' And Purvis had said, 'What am I supposed to do?' And his girl had said, 'I don't know, let's try and push him back out into the water.' They'd bent down and pushed as hard as they could and he'd swam out a bit and got hold of the whale's tail, but it was no good; he was too damn big and heavy, so they just gave up and sat on the sand by his head. Purvis had looked him in his eye and swore to god the whale was telling him something with his eye, but for the life of him he couldn't figure out what it might have been and then his girl had put her hand on the whale's head and said, 'It's alright Purvis, he wants to die and that's what he's gonna do.' So they just sat back down and tried to stroke him and talk to him and his girl had started singing songs and telling him nursery rhymes. When it got dark it seemed like finally it was over because his eye stopped talking, but they didn't leave, they just sat there until the next morning and watched the sun come up and the gulls started landing on the beach and walking over to the whale. He chased them away but they just hopped back over again and his girl had put her arm through his and said, 'Come on Purvis, we got to go,' and they'd climbed back up the cliff and when they got to the top they looked back down to the beach and saw the gulls rowed up on the back of the whale trying to cut through his skin and peck his eyes and just down the beach they saw a small coyote working its way in zig-zags up the sand and heading for the whale. His girl had said, 'No Purvis, I don't want to see this, please let's go.' And he had nodded his head and taken her hand and they'd turned and walked up the small dirt road that led back to the freeway.

That night as he lay in his bed on the ward listening to all the heart monitors beeping and the oxygen tanks hissing and the ventilators rising and falling, rising and falling, Purvis reached over and opened the top drawer on his bedside table and took out a folded up napkin and opened it up on his stomach. He'd been saving up his pills – there was a whole bunch of them. That's gotta be enough, thought Purvis, but then he thought how he would just be another one to go out the back where nobody could see and he shook his head and put the pills back in the drawer and thought to himself, tomorrow morning I'm gonna get a taxi and go back to that beach and I'm gonna swim out in the ocean just as far as I can and then let go, I'm just gonna float and float and float until I can't float no more. Then I'll sink down to the bottom and lay my head on the sand and that will be that. But Purvis knew that really he could never get down those cliffs, he was just kidding him-self. Shit, he was an old man, he could barely make it to the bathroom without needing some help, and then Purvis folded his hands back over his chest and closed his eyes, 'No harm in dreamin',' he whispered to himself and then he thought about how good that cigarette and cup of black coffee was gonna taste in the morning.

The Cambodian

She was sheltering from the rain under the awning of the Eddy Street Hotel, trying to catch her first twenty of the day and across the street, squatting on his haunches in the downpour, was this little Cambodian staring intently up the road. He was waiting to score, she knew right away; every inch of his little being was focused on the few cars that were turning into Eddy from Market with their headlights cutting through the pre-dawn deadness of a Tenderloin morning.

When an old tan Chevy Impala came into view he was up and moving. It passed him then pulled over halfway up the block. He caught up to it and leaned into the driver's side window, then stood up and the Impala was gone.

'Hey,' she called as she crossed the street, 'hey mister, wait, let me talk to you.'

'What you want, lady?'

'I just want to talk to you.'

'Yeah, yeah, what you want?'

As she got up to him she reached out her hand and held his arm. 'Listen mister, I'm sick and I got seven dollars, please let me in on it, I swear to god I'll take care of you later.' The Cambodian looked her over then pulled up the sleeve of her pink fake mohair sweater and looked at the tracks that snaked their way from her wrist on up to her neck.

'Ok, lady, wait here I be back.'

'Here, take the money,' she said and tried to hand him the five and two ones she had rolled up in her left hand.

'Lap don't want your money, lady, Lap say wait here, you wait here, Lap be back, ok? Wait here.'

Ten minutes later and the rain had stopped. She had run out of cigarettes and her stomach was churning when she saw him heading back down Eddy towards her.

He signaled with his hand for her to stay put and with a big smile on his face he reached into the top pocket of his denim suit jacket and pulled out a 100cc syringe, he looked over his shoulder, then, when he got to her, put it down the front of her sweater and laughed – it landed between her breasts.

She walked quickly down to the park on McAllister and ducked in through a hole that had been cut in the chain link fence. She knelt down on the muddy concrete behind the closed public toilet and pulled out the syringe. 35ccs of dark brown liquid; it didn't look like a cotton, it looked like a proper hit. She shook her left hand real fast for a minute, then put it on the ground and stood on it just above the wrist with her right foot, then she popped the orange cap with her teeth and flicked the point of the needle into the tiny vein that ran along the inside of her thumb just above the palm. When she saw the faintest trickle of pink she slowly pushed the plunger all the way down and closed her eyes and waited.

It didn't take long, it was a speedball – the little gook had come through. She flew up with the coke and opened her eyes wide as she gasped for some air and then felt the velvet warmth of the heroin billow out like a parachute to catch her gentle as she spiraled back down. 'Oh, holy Mary,' she whispered, 'thank you, thank you for the blessings we receive, oh, holy mother of Jesus, thank you, thank you, thank you.'

Then she stood up and wiped her hand on the side of her skirt and went back to work.

She saw the Cambodian later that evening strolling down Larkin Street, arm in arm with two Mexican transvestites, a white carnation in the lapel of his bloodstained suit jacket.

'Hello girlie,' he said when she crossed the street heading towards him.

She smiled. 'Hello mister.'

'Lap take care of you good ha, girlie?

She nodded her head. 'You sure did.'

'Lap got the best shit in TL yeah? You want some fat-ass balloon, you come see Lap. You want balloon?'

She nodded her head again and the Cambodian withdrew his arms from the trannies and patted them both on their butts and said, 'See you later, babies. Lap gonna take care of some business.' The trannies laughed and blew him a kiss then walked on into the night.

She had eighty dollars, twenty each from two car blowjobs and forty from an alley date where the guy had fucked her in the ass behind the Pink Pussycat theatre. She'd need to make another twenty for a room and twenty more for her wakeup, but she'd worry about that later. Right now she just wanted to fix, everything else could take care of itself.

'How much you got, girlie?'

'Eighty.'

'I get you packet ten and ten eighty dollar. You sell eight shoot two for free, yeah?'

She shook her head. 'I'm not selling anything, I'm shooting it all.'

'Ha! You selling your ass all night long, stupid girl. You like being whore? Ok, be whore, but I'm telling you selling much better.'

'You're sweet.' She smiled and handed him her eighty dollars.

They walked up through the corners of the Tenderloin, each one staked out with its own trade; the black crack whores around the edges of Market Street, then the pre-op transsexuals on Eddy and Jones and further up to Post Street, where the price grew according to the amount of surgery endured. But when they got to Polk Street it was just rent boys and runaways. She never came up here, no-one was interested.

He held up a hand for her to stop and then he disappeared, so she sat on a bench by Cala Foods and watched the people come out with their shopping bags and head home to make dinner and walk the dog and then watch some TV. She thought, well, I'm living on another planet they don't even know about.

When he appeared again he walked by her whistling,

and she followed him, back down to the piss alleys and the liquor stores and the GA hotels of the TL, stepping over the bodies of drunk Indians sprawled on the sidewalk with bloody noses and swollen livers, past the shopping cart people outside Glide Memorial, waiting for a ten o'clock sandwich.

'Where you stay?' said the Cambodian.

'Right here,' she said and held out her hand for her packet.

'Poor white girl,' he said as he palmed her the ball wrapped in plastic.

'Whadya mean?'

The Cambodian laughed, 'Lap live with mother and grandmother and brothers and sisters. Lap live with family, yeah?'

'So?'

'So, my people stronger than heroin, yeah? Family stronger than heroin. Your people broken, heroin is king daddy. It's ok, girlie, not your fault, you born American. Ha ha ha it's just the dharma,' but she was already gone.

The Window

She was sitting on her blue suitcase in the underground parking lot early in the morning crying her eyes out. She couldn't remember exactly what happened other than she was scared. She had one side of her face raised up, angry and red from the punch, and she couldn't move her right wrist, it just hung there. They'd kicked in the door – that she remembered. It was French Nick and that asshole Hobbit who'd been coming around for the past month to cut and bag in the hotel room. They'd hit Donny on top of his head with a claw hammer and then hung him out the fourth floor window by his ankles. He twisted and screamed and begged and said, 'It wasn't me, please you motherfuckers I swear to god it wasn't me.' Then they'd pulled him up and punched him in the stomach and slapped his face and then hung him back out the window.

She didn't know what they were supposed to have done but she was pretty sure Donny had done it, whatever it was. He was just like that – charming and slimy and full of shit. When she'd tried to get out the front door Hobbit had grabbed her by the hair in the hallway and dragged her back into the room by her wrist and punched her in the face. After that she didn't remember, it was all slow motion. 'I'm gonna sit here a while then I'm gonna go make some money,' she said out loud to herself. 'I'm gonna go make some money and get my own hotel room where nobody knows me and I'm never gonna see Donny again, that asshole motherfucker, I hope they kill him that fuckin' creep, that lying rat bastard.' Then she ran out of breath and started crying again.

When a few cars started coming down the ramp from the street and parking up she figured it must have been about eight o'clock. She kept her face down so no-one could say, 'What happened to you?' or 'Are you alright?' and dragged the suitcase up the ramp and out onto Capp Street. She crossed over to a pay phone on the corner of 17th and pushed zero for the operator.

'Hi, I want to make a collect call please. Yeah it's 415 345 8085, my name's Tracy and the calls for Deborah. Ok, thank you'. She waited a while. 'Hi mom, no I know I'm sorry, I've been busy. Mom I need you to help me out. No everything's ok, it's just the cat's real sick and I need to take her to the vets right now and I don't get paid 'till Friday, mom. No I know I owe you and I swear on Friday I'll pay you everything, ok? Ok, no Western Union. Yeah, two hundred. Yeah. No not later on mom, I need it now. Just use your credit card. Please mom, Puffin's so sick and I'm scared she's gonna die. Ok. Ok, thanks mom. Oh, thank you mom! Ok I love you too, I'll call you back in twenty minutes to get the secret number. Ok. Is dad ok? Oh, I'm sorry. Ok I'm gonna go ok? Please do it quick. Ok thanks mom. Yeah I love you too.'

When she put the phone down she felt better. She opened the suitcase and dug around for her little red leather pouch she kept her ID inside and just for a moment she panicked, but then there it was. She tucked it into the inside pocket of her fake leather jacket and then winced because her wrist hurt a lot. She took out her hairbrush and tried to straighten out her hair with her left hand, but it felt clumsy and wrong and she wondered how in the world she was gonna do her mascara.

The Cellmates

At six fifteen the call went out for chow unlock in West Block tiers one and two. 'Chow time, chow time, move your asses.' He was on the fourth tier – that gave him ten minutes. He stood by the bars and buttoned up his carrot suit and slipped into the size ten-and-a-half jap flaps he'd ended up in after he sold his sneakers. He'd been awake since four listening to the call-out list for transportation. Nothing. He'd been in state reception four months and county for three and his time hadn't even started yet – that was the bitch of an n-number. Slinging his orange jacket over his shoulder he gripped the bars and did some more calf raises– he'd already busted out 500 push-ups and 300 crunches and he was hungry. He had a fake medical pass slung around his neck and when the gate slid open he was going hunting.

'Travis is a piece of shit Travis is a piece of shit yeah yeah we know.'

Fourth tier unlock.

The bolt pulled back and fifty cell doors ground open and ninety nine orange-clad convicts headed to the wrought iron stairwell to join the 300 below, all lined up under the gaze of the gunners on the catwalk above.

He'd had the cell to himself for four days. No celly was good news – he liked to be alone. He must have seen ten men come and go in the four months he'd been waiting, only one of them worth remembering – that youngster with the colostomy bag. The kid used to stay in on unlocks, skip meals and go hungry so he could have the cell to himself when he washed out the shit from the tubes and the plastic sack that he strapped to his stomach. It took a week for the kid to even tell him why he was skipping meals and when he did he'd shaken his head and said, 'Come to chow you stupid motherfucker, I'm starving. If you won't eat it I will and we can sell the bag lunch for tobacco. I don't give a fuck what it smells like, ok?' The kid had nodded his head but when they got to chow and the kid handed him his tray he'd said, 'Eat the shit, man, just give me the cookies and Kool-Aid from the bag lunch so I can get us some fuckin' tobacco.'

He liked the kid. He was quiet at night and he'd sit still on the top bunk reading a bible and then he'd write long letters to his mother. He never hung his legs over the edge of the bunk so his feet dangled in his face and sometimes early in the morning he would hear him crying real softly in his sleep. He usually never asked what people were in for but with the kid he couldn't help it.

'So why are you here, man. What the fuck did you do?'

The kid was quiet for a while and then said, 'I stole a car and ran over a lady and she died.'

'Why the fuck did you do that?'

The kid shook his head slowly then said gently, 'I think

I wanted to crash into a wall, but I can't remember.'

'You wanted to crash into a wall?'

'Yeah.'

'Why?'

'I dunno, it seemed like the right thing to do.'

'Listen, kid, don't tell nobody that shit, ok? You stole a car end of story, got it?'

The kid nodded his head then looked him in the eyes for a while.

'Why?' he said.

''Cos they'll fuckin' eat you alive.'

Out in the yard it was San Quentin cold. The gulls flapped around the trashcans, fighting over crusts and some trustees dressed in state blue were smoking in a circle, talking shit and trying to see if there was any business to be had from the orange stream of new fish heading into breakfast.

'Envelopes for sneakers,' they called.

'Half a can for your Reeboks, homeboy.'

'Hey, I got two-for-one canteen, come on, you know you're fuckin' hungry. Come and get it, fish. Ha ha ha.'

In the chow hall he ate quickly then spun around low until he caught up with the first tier that was already heading back. When the cop threw him his bag lunch he tucked it down the front of his jumpsuit and walked another ten yards, then broke rank and headed to where the sergeant was running the callouts from the main obs at the intersection of the block runs. He flashed the medical pass that hung around his neck and the sergeant waved him through. Just before x-ray he saw a line of carrot suits heading in to chow. East Block? North Block? He couldn't tell, but as long as it wasn't PCs it didn't matter. He waited until he saw some white faces then about-faced and squeezed into the ranks.

'Sorry homey, on a mission,' he replied to the grunt of the convict he'd stepped in front of. 'What Block you from?' he asked.

'East Block.'

'Cool man, thanks,' he said, and knew he could probably catch North Block on the way out if he was fast.

Half an hour later he had four bag lunches tucked around the sides of his jumpsuit and he was full to overflowing on ground beef and gravy and milk biscuits. He headed back through to the yard heading for West Block, limping for effect and holding his medical pass in front of him like it was the Holy Grail.

'Travis is a piece of shit Travis smokes after niggers Travis is a tore up motherfucker with no back up Travis is a snipe rat.'

He entered the cave of West Block, walked up to the cop at the control desk, held out his pass and said, 'Claxton N62613 fourth tier, back from medical.' The cop pointed to the yellow box painted on the floor and went back to reading his newspaper.

West Block was a zoo. The sound of 500 caged men shouting and laughing and swearing bounced off the cement hanger that was built over the cellblock itself. Every so often a wave of animal calls would sweep over the inmates and they'd stand at the face of their cells holding the bars with their heads thrown back, baying like donkeys, neighing like horses or crowing like roosters until the moment passed. At five o'clock when the call for psych meds came over the PA the whole block opened up again with a rousing chorus of 'Cuckoo, cuckoo, cuckoo, motherfuckin' J cats, cuckoo.' He'd been here five times now – you got used to it – yep, you could pretty much get used to anything.

When he got back to his cell he saw a fat guy sitting on his bunk holding his state issue blanket and spare jumpsuit in a pile on his lap just like he'd received it. As he waited for the cop to key him in he leaned into the bars of the cell and said, 'What you doing on my bunk man? Yours is on top.' The fat guy looked at him through a thick pair of glasses, dropped his head to the left and just said, 'Oh.' Slowly he stood up and placed his bundle on to the bare mattress on top. He was huge – at least six four and 300 pounds, but he was soft. You could tell at a glance that he was soft as baby shit but Travis knew that was the kind of guy who was probably here for chopping off his mother's head or eating his little sister.

His name was Ripley. He introduced himself like he was at the country club, holding out a chubby hand that Travis just looked at. Ripley was fat, but Ripley was smart. By the end of the second night he'd covered the ceiling with most of the visible universe, first in pencil and when that ran out in the chalk Travis had stolen from the cop station. Travis sat on a blanket folded across the steel toilet and watched him work. They'd been on lockdown since the first morning Ripley had arrived – that meant no movement and all meals were bag lunches delivered by a few lifer trustees twice a day. The blue light above North Block was lit. Somebody was on deathwatch.

Ripley said that only eleven people had actually been executed in the state of California since the reintroduction of the death penalty in 1973 and that America was in the throes of a longstanding war upon itself and that all technology was just a cover for the innate desire of the human psyche to eradicate itself. He used his fingers in the light coming off the gunners' catwalk to cast shadows on the back of the cell wall to illustrate the allegory of Plato's dwellers in the cave. When he felt safe enough he leaned close to Travis and whispered that 'thought is the real obstacle to freedom' and that 'the only logical path was to develop choiceless awareness through years of self-discipline and the rejection of all authority including your own.' Travis nodded his head and said, 'Ok, but just keep your distance man, you're getting a little bit too close.' Ripley stood up straight and nodded his head in agreement.

Early on the third morning when Travis got up to do his work out he found Ripley sitting cross-legged on his bunk with his glasses off and his hands extended on his knees with his thumbs touching his forefingers.

Travis said, 'What the fuck are you doing, man?' And after a long exhale Ripley replied, 'I'm piercing the bull's nostrils and bringing the seven horses of the senses into line with the will of the chariot driver.'

Travis was quiet for a while then said, 'Do you have any money on your books?' Ripley nodded his head.

'How much?'

'Two thousand.'
'That'll do,' said Travis and started his push-ups.

The Pavement

The cart was almost full when he collapsed. He'd been out since midnight picking through the trash in the dumpsters in the alleys behind the restaurants and the bars. Brown glass, aluminum cans, clear glass, green glass – he had everything in a kind of order up and down the cart. Aluminum was best, clear glass was next, the rest was just pennies but it all added up. He knew what had happened but it was too late to do anything about it now.

His stomach churned and he was squirting hot water out of his ass and it felt like he had to breath fifty times real fast to pull in one breath. When he'd gone down he'd just laid there, staring level with the pavement to where it dropped off into the road. It was kind of peaceful, like somehow he'd been given permission to stop for a while and now all he could do was lie there and wait until it passed.

'Twelve dollars,' he groaned, 'it's gotta be about twelve dollars now,' and he reached out a hand to grab a wheel on the bottom of the cart and pull it over close to where he was lying. As long as the cart was there everything would be all right. 'Twelve dollars,' he said again and closed his eyes.

It was August and hot and the field was dry. He opened the gate in the redwood fence that separated the back-yard from the open field and stepped onto the snake grass. His dog ran ahead of him sniffing in circles and wagging its tail in excitement. They set out for the small arroyo just before the freeway. As he walked he opened the tube of BBs he had stolen that morning from the hard-ware store in Crystal Springs and poured them into the chamber of his daisy air rifle – his mom had bought it for him at Gemco on his thirteenth birthday in July. He wasn't supposed to use it without adult supervision, but she was always working and his dad had been gone now for over a year. They crossed the fire line that had been cut into the field to save the houses from burning and passed under the towers of the electrical pylons that ran up the coast forever. By the first trees were some boulders with empty cans of Coors and Budweiser bottles scattered around them. The high school kids came out here on Friday nights and got drunk and raced their mini-bikes and sometimes set fire to the grass. He put three cans on top of a boulder and stepped out twenty paces, then spun fast and fired. He hit the first two dead on, but just nicked the third – he thought it might fall but it didn't. He pumped up the rifle and closed in slowly and shot the can off the boulder, then kept firing and pumping until it was just a mangled bit of scrap.

His dog started to bark over by the scrub forest and he filled the rifle again as he walked down to see what was there. It was a gopher snake, about three feet long. The dog had it trapped in the grass in front of a set of rocks. He called the dog back and took aim and fired. He hit it just behind the head but it didn't seem to do anything but stun it. Walking closer and pumping the rifle as tight as he could, he put the barrel to the head of the snake, about three inches away and pulled the trigger. The snake's head split open and it thrashed its tail forward and it came off the ground then lay still.

He sat in the dirt by the snake and opened a ten-cent packet of sunflower seeds he had in his pocket and filled his mouth, splitting them open using his tongue and his teeth and spitting out the shells. He thought about the bird he had killed last week, how it had fallen from the branches of the tree and then run in circles on the ground with one wing flapping, the other one broken from where it had been hit by the pellet. He'd shot it again but it just kept running in circles. It took twelve shots to finally make it lie down and die.

He settled onto his back and looked up at the blue ocean of sky. He could feel his lungs filling up with each breath he took and how they dropped slowly when he exhaled. As he lay there it seemed like the grass around him was coming alive, he didn't know how, but he could feel it growing and he wondered if he'd been an Indian in some other lifetime and if he'd been in this very same field before the pylons or houses or police helicopters and if he'd been brave and been able to bring down a mule deer with one arrow and skin it with his knife and bring home the meat slung over his back and if his family had been waiting for him and if they'd let out cheers and whoops when he came into view because they were hungry and he was the one they counted on to bring them food.

When he woke up the dog was licking his face and whining. It was getting dark. As he sat up he decided he wasn't going home, he wanted to spend the night out here with his rifle and his dog and the Indian ghosts.

By nine o'clock it was black and the stars spread out above him. He knew he was going to be in trouble but he didn't care. He headed down to the fence line at the end of the field and looked out over the freeway to the reservoir on the other side. He wanted to be over there on the shore, he wanted to sleep next to the water with just him and the night, but there was no way across the freeway – it was a twenty foot drop to the road. The freeway had been cut through the hills thirty years ago and ran six lanes wide on both sides all the way to San Jose or up to San Francisco. He pumped up his rifle and took a bead on a car in the slow lane below him. 'No way would the pellet reach that,' he said and pulled the trigger.

At first nothing happened, then he saw the car veer over into the next lane and clip the side of a pickup truck. Then it swung back into the slow lane with the tires smoking as the driver tried to brake. It pulled up a quarter mile down onto the shoulder. He was breathing fast. He crouched down on his haunches with the rifle in his hands and moved like a wolf in the darkness on the ridge above the freeway. When he got above the car he saw a lady standing to the front of the bonnet waving her hands for someone to stop. He saw the shattered window on the front passengers side where his shot had hit. He could just make out a small child in the backseat staring out the window straight at him. He ducked down and pumped his rifle then stood up and fired away at the lady's head. She yelped like a hurt puppy, clutched the back of her skull with her hands and dropped to her knees on the asphalt.

When he got to the gate of his backyard he felt strong and calm. He dug a small trench in the dirt of the field with his fingers then he wrapped the rifle in a sheet of plastic that he tore from the length along the bottom of the fence line that his father had laid to keep the gophers out and buried it. He crossed the overgrown lawn at the back of the house, slid open the glass door and stepped quietly inside.

When the sun started creeping up he was still lying there. He didn't know how long it had been but he'd stopped puking and squirting and now he was just shaking real bad. People's shoes started to walk by his head and car tires spun by in the road but he stared straight on and thought pretty soon he was gonna be able to get up and get going again.

'I've eaten bad shit, I've eaten bad shit an' I got food poisoning. I guess I'm only human after all.'

When the ambulance came he was sitting up and was just about to get to his feet.

The doors opened and two paramedics climbed out of the cab and walked over to him, one of them was drinking a cup of coffee and he held up his hand and said, 'I'm ok fellas, yup I'm ok,' and the paramedics just stood there and watched him as he slowly climbed to his feet and put his forearms on the cart's handlebar and started slowly down the pavement to the recycling center.

As he got nearer he could see the gulls riding up in the air from off the mountains of trash and he could hear the hydraulics on the crushers and the roar of the dozers. He felt his strength coming back – it started from his feet and worked its way up his legs and through his guts then washed clear up through his head and he thought it was a good time for a song, so he cleared his throat and spat and then he started to sing.

The Mouse

When Rainey de Soto shot speed she kind of blacked out and when she came to the only thing she could be pretty sure of was that she'd probably been fucking a lot of guys. She'd been that way since she could remember, and if she came to with money in her pocket, well that was good, but if she was broke it was ok too, she'd just have to start fucking again, but this time she would try to pay attention.

When Rainey was thirteen she'd got on the back of a Harley one afternoon and ended up locked in a closet for three months inside an old trailer that sat on the edge of the desert. At first she was scared, but then she got used to it and when they started shooting her up to test out the new batch of meth that they'd cooked in another trailer that sat further out in the wasteland she found that she didn't really have a problem with whatever they wanted to do to her, it was just easier that way.

They called her the mouse and they took her on rides to do business with the Mexicans, or the nomads, or whoever had the cash, and after the deal was done and if everything went smooth she got handed around with the whiskey and the syringes. She got pretty good at what she did and they even started fighting over her; a couple of guys got stabbed and one fella got it in the chest with a shotgun when he tried to say he was taking her for himself. Ace and Dago had got pretty pissed off and rode after them and Ace had pulled up ahead of them and turned around with the shotgun pointed straight at the man's chest and pulled the trigger. The bike had dropped and spun out sparks and she got her jaw broken and her ribs cracked, but when Ace had driven up to where she was lying and sat her behind him and pulled away with her holding on tight, she had to admit she was pretty pleased with all the attention.

But now everybody was in prison. She'd been in prison too, but then she'd turned state's witness, cut a deal and she'd testified and got given sixteen months while everybody else got twenty years and when she was released after doing twelve they transported her to 850 Bryant Street and gave her some ID and two hundred bucks. They pushed the buzzer on the door and she stepped out onto the streets, all alone for the first time since she was a kid.

'I ain't fuckin' no more bikers,' she vowed as she walked up the block holding a see-through plastic bag in her hand with a few bits of clothing inside that they'd given her at the jailhouse. 'I ain't fuckin' no bikers and I ain't fuckin' no niggers. I'm just gonna fuck normal people for a change.' In fact, thought Rainey, as the new possibilities of a free world dawned on her, in fact I'm gonna get a good man to look after me and I'm gonna be faithful and I'm gonna go to college and I might even have a baby and I'm gonna be a good mom and raise him right and teach him not to tell lies and how to be kind to people and, and… but first I'm gonna get a little bit of speed, and then Rainey stopped and stood still with her eyes closed and her heart started beating fast and the palms of her hands began sweating as she ran her tongue around the inside of her gums and over her teeth and she swore to god that somehow she could taste it already.

The Tree

Indio smoked in a tree. He just climbed up that trunk like he was invisible and settled down in the branches and got out his pipe while the whole world walked by underneath, oblivious.

Indio was up in his tree, right there on 16th and Mission, smack bang in the middle of the zone where hundreds of people walk by: good people, bad people, nobody people, cop people, rich people, poor people. There were fucking people everywhere, but he was all alone, up in that tree.

The first time I saw him up there I laughed and thought, that crazy fucker. I could see him through the leaves just smiling down at me and he put his finger to his mouth and goes, 'Hush.'

Indio had come over from Cuba as a kid with the Marielitos. He told me he grew up deep in the country on a sugar cane plantation and he said his hands had been like bark since he could walk from working the fields. He was a handsome man like an Arab Valentino from old Hollywood movies, like John Garfield with pockmarks all over his face. He'd been a boxer for who knows how long, forever perhaps. You could tell by his presence; he moved like a stallion and that's what he was, a beautiful stallion in a land of donkeys and mules.

You know I get things fucked up, my memories all over the place, but about that night I remember. It's like they were shooting *Apocalypse Now* all over again, like it was real, but at the same time everyone's just going through the motions.

So it's dusk and getting darker and I'm standing watch for my girl standing there on 16th staring down to Capp Street, hoping she'll turn the corner with forty dollars in her hand. I got a little dime of rock so every now and then I duck up to Valencia where I got a pipe stuck above a door frame and I take it down and get a hit, then I go back down to make sure she doesn't get away.

Indio's been up in his tree and everything's normal but then on my last lap something's changed, it's different. Indio's not up in the tree anymore, he's kind of sitting in this weird position up on the end of the railings that go around the BART station entrance, fifteen feet high. He's kind of hanging there leaning over, but he doesn't cry out or anything, he's just hanging there breathing hard, so I pass underneath and I see it, he's fallen out the tree and got skewered on the end of the railings that curve up and out with these fucking spears on the top – they're made for a medieval castle, like stakes for a vampire. The architects must have thought they looked impressive running round the BART station entrance, but why they needed them I don't know. Indio is completely impaled through his right thigh, you can see the tip of the spear coming up out of his leg and he's not going anywhere, but that fucker doesn't make a sound, he just grits his teeth and breathes real hard now and then.

'Indio, what the fuck?' I say.

'I'm stuck man, I can't get down,' he says, then some lady sees me looking up at him and she raises her head and then she covers her mouth with her hand and starts crying, 'Oh my god, oh my god.'

Someone calls the fire brigade and the police cars arrive and they set up big spotlights and torches and flares to keep people away, but there's people everywhere and they're all standing in a big circle with their hands over their mouths as the firemen set up ladders and the ambulances are there and after a while they get out a big chainsaw and start it up. The noise roars through the night and these sparks start flying up into the sky as they try to cut down the railings with the spear still through his leg. It was taking them a long time so every now and then I'd walk back up to Valencia Street and take another hit on my pipe, but the rock's almost gone and there's no sign of my girl and I'm walking back down to the movie set and they're on take twenty-two and he's still just hanging there in the night sky, with his eyes shining like a crazy star over the Mission. But hey, here comes that girl, about fucking time.

It was about a year later I saw him shuffling down Mission Street he looked smaller somehow. He smiled and held out his hand and I said, 'Jesus man, what fuckin' happened that night?' And he laughed and told me how they had cut the pole with the chainsaw and lifted him down with it still through his leg and how he'd laid on his side in the ambulance and they took him to SF General straight into surgery and when he woke up it was out but he was in the jail ward because they figured out who he was and that he had warrants and he'd just been released from San Bruno the day before and one of his homies had fronted him a quarter ounce to get him going and did I need anything? 'Yeah, yeah sure, I'll take a twenty, amigo,' I said, and he reached into his mouth and spat out a red balloon and put it in my hand and I paid him a twenty and shook his hand again and walked back up to Valencia to the steps I used to fix on and got out my cooker and syringe and opened up the red balloon and inside was this piece of tree bark just sitting there where the heroin was supposed to be and I thought, isn't that great, I guess we are even now, because that night I'd just walked away, no, not really, ha, I thought, that fucking piece of shit Cuban dog fucker, lucky I got another twenty.

The Doorway

It was more like a patio than a doorway. It came up six steps from the street and then opened out into a kind of a cave, mosaicked with dolphins and starfish and little Indians paddling canoes. The good thing about it was that when you lay up on the side wall by the front door of the building, the only thing showing would be from your knees down to your feet. In the time they'd been sleeping there nobody had come up to move them on, or arrest them, or check them for warrants.

She'd always had a boyfriend or someone she looked after and right now it was a deaf kid from Oklahoma who she called Joey. Joey was good company because he didn't steal her cottons or try to beat her up. He just watched her gently like she was his mom or his sister and he was kind of good looking in a weird way, with long, black hair, parted in the middle, and his skin was brown and soft all over.

At night Joey would go up and down the neighborhood checking the black bags left outside the thrift stores for clean blankets and jackets and little pillows that they could sleep on and he always brought back old pastries and donuts for her to eat. At first they'd been having sex but lately they just curled up together when she was too tired to keep working.

In the beginning when she'd got into a car to do a date, Joey would try to run along the sidewalk and keep up with them and she'd have to roll down the window and lean out and yell, 'Stay there you stupid motherfucker, I'll be back,' and even though he couldn't hear her when she got back a little bit later Joey would be standing in the same spot and she'd say, 'Come on, let's go get well.' Joey would follow her up the street to Valencia and she'd get a one and one and a nickel of rock and they would duck down the little alley across from the projects and sit on the ground behind some parked car and tear the bottom off a beercan and cook up the chiva and sprinkle the coke on top of it and pull it up in two syringes and she always gave Joey half, holding the syringes up together above her eyes to make sure there was exactly the same amount in each barrel.

She kept the rock for herself – that was something that she made clear. 'The rock's for me,' she'd say slowly. 'Do you understand?' and Joey would grin and shrug his shoulders and try to look away so she could smoke it in peace.

They couldn't go to the doorway until after six o'clock in the evening because it was a community center for mentally retarded people, and then they had to be gone by nine every morning. But the people who worked there knew that they slept in the doorway because sometimes they came to work a bit early and they'd be still sleeping. The first time they'd seen them a lady had said, 'Excuse me, can we get through,' and they'd sat up and moved aside and the lady had gone up and unlocked the door and then turned around and said, 'Listen, if you guys keep this spot clean I don't mind you sleeping here but you have to be gone before our clients arrive and please don't leave any needles lying around, ok?' and she'd said, 'Ok,' and the lady had smiled at her and then gone inside the building.

It was nice to have a place where you were allowed to be at, and they kept the doorway clean and rolled up their blankets and folded up the flats of cardboard in the morning before they left and Joey would hide them behind a dumpster down the street. But sometimes at night when they came back the blankets would be gone and Joey would have to go find some more, but that was ok because there was always plenty around, you just had to know where to look for them.

One afternoon around five she got a hundred bucks from an old guy in a pick up truck who said he was looking for his granddaughter who'd run away a long time ago and he showed her a picture of a girl with brown hair and green eyes and she'd said, 'Nope, I ain't seen her,' and the old man had said, 'If you see her can you tell her to call her mother please,' and she had said, 'Yeah,' and the man had opened his wallet and given her five twenties and let her out. She hadn't even had to do anything with him and she'd run back to find Joey thinking that today was gonna be a good day and they'd gone up to find the El Salvadorian who sold ten and tens for seventy bucks, but he hadn't been in his spot. Somebody else was there and he sold them a packet and she'd said, 'Fuck it,' and gone and rented them a room at the Van Ness Motel with the other thirty because it wasn't six o'clock yet, and when they opened the balloons the chiva looked different, not like it was supposed to – it was all powdery crystals. But when they put it in the cooker and squirted some water on it and put the lighter underneath it smelled like it was chiva after all, so they pulled up two big shots with three dimes of coke inside and she got to work looking for a vein in her fingers and when she looked up Joey was laying still on the carpet with the needle hanging out of the top of his ankle where he fixed at.

'Joey,' she'd said but his eyes were closed and she knew, but she tried not to think about it until she had got a register and when she did she pushed in the plunger thinking, I don't care anyway, and then her head had caught on fire and she leaned over jerking like somebody was kicking her around the floor.

When she came to it was so quiet in the room, she had tried to wake Joey up and she shook him and slapped his face and tried to breath in his mouth and then she'd punched him in his chest a few times and then she gave up and looked at him again for a bit and then she'd reached over and pulled the syringe out of his ankle because it was still half full and she stuck it in the top pocket of her jean jacket and then stepped out of the motel room.

The Surgeon

At six am in March the sun comes up outta the eastern foothills of Hayward and Alameda County in perfection and rolls back the purple robe of twilight's last gleaming into the cold waters of the northern Pacific and sends it on its way. The crows hop down from their branches in the oak trees of Dolores Park and sit around the rims of the trashcans that line the green sloping grass hill outside the old Mission and caw out the mysteries of want and despair into the unsuspecting eardrums of sleeping vagrants who lay curled up on flats of cardboard set atop the wooden benches that were erected for the asses of good citizens who may wish to take a load off come weekend, or on the occasional evening stroll after a long hard day's work. Grady suffered the cold with patience, sprawled out on the wooden planks that were never intended for the likes of he. Flotsam and jetsam? No, you got to sweep it up as progress moves on in the grip of its never-ending quest to hide its imperfections from itself.

'It's a goddamned shame,' said Grady to himself as he realized he'd woken up again and that he was no longer drunk. Then he sat up and spat and straightened his spine and opened his eyes. I need a drink, he thought, and that ain't no illusion, I need a drink right now or else I'm gonna be sick as a fucking pig, and that my friend is a physical fact, yep there's no fucking theory involved in that little pearl… Grady reached over and grabbed his old trainers from the end of the bench where they'd served as a pillow and pulled them over the grey sludge that covered his feet that once upon a time had been the pair of socks he'd put on the morning he'd walked out of Atascadero State mental hospital thirty days ago now, with his discharge papers tucked into his back pocket.

'I need some dollars an' cents, I need some nickels an' some dimes an' some quarters so's I can concentrate on the task at hand,' which was for Grady to get his body to stop shaking for long enough so that he could operate. Grady had been operating on himself for 38 years now, peeling back the skin on his forearms to take a look inside, slicing through the soft underbelly of his wrists with razors to let out some pressure, or else banging his head against the concrete walls of his jail cells so that he could evoke a change in his state of mind or just knock himself out for a bit. 'I'm a psychic surgeon,' said Grady to no-one in particular, least of all the doctors who wrote and rewrote his prescriptions of Olanzapine and MAO inhibitors and Citalopram in an effort to find that perfect balance. 'Well, he's definitely bipolar and we believe it's likely that he's been suffering from post traumatic stress since childhood as a result of prolonged beatings inflicted by his father, and then he comes out positive on the Hare Checklist for sociopathic tendencies. The only mystery here is that he hasn't killed anybody yet, at least that we know about.'

At ten o'clock each morning Grady would get to his spot outside Kentucky Fried Chicken on Mission Street and place a red bandana on the pavement just in front of him, then kneel down like he was praying and hold still for as long as it took for three dollars to accumulate out of the sky. He never looked up or to the side or said thank you or please, he just froze like he was a gargoyle perched on top of Notre Dame Cathedral. The only time that Grady flinched was if kids came by and stared at him. Kids made him have to work that much harder – all it took was a little laugh or an innocent eye to meet his and a trap door would spring open in the bottom of Grady's guts and a big green python would leap up out of its cave, shoot the length of Grady's spine and smash its tail around the edges of his skull trying to get out and wrap itself around the windpipe of whatever kid had woken it up from its slumber. Then Grady would start rocking back and forth making strange growls and rolling his eyes as he fought with all of the goodness that was left inside him against the raging.

Grady had come to the conclusion that the only thing for it was for him to stay as drunk as possible for as long as he could and for the time in-between to be devoted to getting the means to start over again. When he was drunk Grady just knew he was a good guy, he wouldn't hurt nobody, shit he would just lay on the pavement passed out in his own piss as people stepped over him, or sometimes spat on him or even occasionally set his pants on fire.

'I am a ghost farm' Grady wrote to himself as he sat on his bench at midnight beneath the rolling black canopy that was his universe, punctuated by stars that, perhaps, no longer even existed.

　'I am a ghost farm
　I am a ghost farm
　I am a ghost farm
　I am a ghost fa…'

The Runner

Angel was all fucked up. She had this thing when she shot coke – she had to take off all of her clothes because she thought they were gonna catch fire then she'd get out this little razor blade from her purse and she'd start doing surgery on her arms and her legs.

'What the fuck are you doing, Angel?' I'd say.

'My body's full of bugs man, they're everywhere inside me and I got to get them out.'

'Angel there's no bugs in your body, you're just paranoid.'

Then she'd grind her teeth together and get out this folded up piece of paper she'd torn from a kid's science book and hold it out for you to read. It said: 'Each human body contains four pounds of microbes, living organisms that have created a niche for themselves inside us, all part of the wonderful world of nature.' And you'd say 'Wow.' And she'd look real serious and take back the piece of paper and say, 'See what I mean?' and then you'd just kind of let her get on with it.

Angel lived in this burnt out car behind the railroad tracks on 3rd Street. I used to go down there with my pipe and I'd break her off a crumb and sit in the back seat beside her and we'd smoke and she'd talk about weird shit like how she could sometimes see the spirits of bad people floating above their heads, how they made a strange sound like a million flies buzzing around a toilet bowl.

Sometimes when we were smoking she'd look over at me like she expected me to kiss her but I never did, but, you know, if we'd shot enough heroin I'd let her lean into my chest and she'd wrap her skinny arms around my waist and lay her head into my shoulder and she'd start humming these little kiddie songs. She said her mom used to sing them to her and she'd forgotten them for so long, but now they were all coming back. At first it would be nice because she had a sweet little voice, but then I'd start feeling like maybe something was wrong and I'd take her arms off me and push her head back up straight and climb out of the car and she'd say,

'Where are you going?' And I'd say,

'I don't know, I just gotta go.' And she'd say,

'Ok' and I'd shut the door and head back up to Mission.

Angel had the virus, but so did a lot of people back then. She used to go round with this Indian kid from Oklahoma who drew pictures of horses and eagles in chalk on the sidewalk while he was waiting for her to come back from doing a trick. When he'd overdosed with the needle still in his arm Angel had just pulled it out and finished the shot.

Angel was a runner. That meant she worked for the Mexicans down on 16th and Mission – she brought them customers and watched out for the cops, and for every three that Angel sold they'd give her one for free.

'Are you looking? Are you looking?' She'd call up and down Mission Street seven days a week, twenty four hours a day.

'Are you looking to score? Do you need something? Chiva, coca, chiva, coca. Hey man, are you looking or what?'

I was never a runner. I was always in a hurry so I found other things that worked for me. One night I got a purse from a lady in a fur coat up outside the opera house and inside the purse next to all the money and the checkbook and the credit cards was this driver's license with Angel's face on it. I showed it to George who was driving.

'George, look at this.'

'Fuck man, that's Angel!'

'It sure fuckin' is, we've got to go get her and clean her up,' I said.

So that's what we did. We drove down to Angel's burnt out car and gave her a dime of rock and said, 'Come with us,' and we rented a room with a shower up on 14th and Valencia, and George went upstairs and got some clothes from some old hooker we knew and we cleaned her up and made her comb her hair and we put her in these straight clothes and threw her old shit in the trashcan. Then we showed her the driver's license and made her start practicing the signature. 'Leona Ward, Leona Ward, Leona Ward.' And Angel started looking through the purse and found these photos of two kids with Leona and then a picture of her husband and a dog and she was saying out loud, 'Leona Ward' and staring at the photo on the driver's license.

We started with the gas stations and cartons of cigarettes, then up to Cala Foods in the Castro and bottles of Courvoisier and Johnny Walker Red Label and Angel was a pro and getting better every time. We didn't fuck around with fences, we went straight to the dealers and then back to the hotel room to fix, then got back in the car and did it again. The next morning we were still running and hit Neiman Marcus and the Emporium and she was flashing that plastic and we got dresses and jackets and Calvin Klein, but we knew that card was about to burn out – each time she flashed it could have been the last. And then it happened. We were in the car out front of Macy's and Angel came running out of the store with two security behind her and we threw open the door and she dove in on top of me. George stepped on the gas and a fucking security man stepped in front of the car and we hit him and he came flying up on the windscreen, trying to hold on like a fucking ten-dollar-an-hour hero. His fingers were wrapped in the window so I punched his hand real hard and he let go and went spinning down Market Street behind us.

'Well Angel, that's it girl,' I said. 'Fun's over, throw that purse away.'

She climbed in the back seat, holding the purse real tight against her breasts and shaking her head and saying, 'No, I'm going to keep this.'

And George said, 'No you're not, you stupid bitch, 'cos if you get stopped you'll get us done with your crazy big mouth, so give me that purse or I'm gonna break your jaw.'

'Calm down George,' I said, and climbed in the back with Angel and said to her real soft:

'Listen honey, you can keep the pictures of the kids and the dog and even the husband but we're gonna get rid of the cards and the checkbook and the ID, ok?' And she just looked out the other window like she was ignoring me and I put my hand up to her cheek real gently and I could see she was crying and I was quiet for a while. Then she nodded her head and handed me the purse.

'Say goodbye Leona,' George said, thinking it's funny and I said:

'Shut up man,' and took out the photos and lipstick and this little charm bracelet with silver hearts on it and put them in Angel's hand. George pulled up by a dumpster on Harrison and I got out the car to hide the purse under the trash and we took Angel back down to her burnt out car and I even opened the door for her to get out then said, 'Thanks, that was fun.' And she said, 'Yeah.'

The Pilot

'Hey kid, do me a favor. Take this five bucks, go over to the liquor store and buy me a pack of Old Golds, ok? Keep the change.'

'Sure thing,' said the kid. He was back in five minutes and handed the pack of cigarettes into the rolled down window of the white Ford Econoline van.

'Here you go.'

''Ata boy,' said the pilot, 'want a drink?'

'Yeah, sure,' said the kid.

'Come on little cowboy,' said the pilot, 'climb on board.'

The van stank of dying animals. It had a grey shagpile carpet that went from the floor to its roof and all the back windows had been covered over with tin foil. On a red pillow on top of the engine mount sat a pink, hairless Chihuahua that sneezed and then growled at the kid as he opened the door and got into the passenger seat. 'Ha, that's Syphilis,' said the pilot. 'He don't like to get cold, motherfucker's been on that engine for three years and I never once turned it off. Here have a drink.' He handed the kid a half empty bottle of Spanada wine and said, 'Roll up your window man,' then turned his head over his left shoulder and shouted into the darkness at the back of the van, 'Hey Jimmy, fix us a joint.' The kid peered into the back and could just make out a fat boy lying on his stomach on top of a mattress, counting change into piles in front of him. 'That's Jimmy, he's my boy. He can't talk but he's a good-un, ain't you Jimmy, you little cocksucker. Here kid, you like country music?' The kid shrugged his shoulders. 'Well, that's all we're gonna play when you're in my motor, got that?' The kid nodded and the pilot pushed a button on the eight-track.

They drove down to the pier and took a left onto the boulevard, heading north towards seaside with George Jones and Tammy Wynette playing live at the Grand Ole Opry. When they got to the checkpoint at Fort Ord the pilot rolled down his window and spat. 'Motherfuckin' pussies,' he said and laughed, 'fuckin' army faggots,' and then turned up towards the marina.

'I'm gonna let you off up here,' said the pilot, 'I got some things to take care of.' 'Ok,' said the kid, and was quiet as the pilot pulled up by the McDonald's drive through. When the van had stopped the kid opened his door and jumped out and as the van was pulling away the kid shouted:

'How come you got no legs?'

''Cos I don't need 'em,' yelled the pilot.

'No seriously man, what happened to your legs?'

The pilot slowed the van down and leaned out of the passenger window and said with a smile, 'I got bored and cut 'em off.' Then he was gone.

It was two nights later as he was moping along the

pier looking for cigarette butts and checking the parking meters for change that he saw the van again. It was pulled up in the last parking spot before the sea with its engine running; you could just make out the dim light coming through the edges of the tinfoil. He walked over to the front of the van and stood looking down at the waves breaking around the faces of the pylons that held up the pier and pretended to be interested. The pilot rolled down his window and called him over.

'What's up, little cowboy? What you doing out here at this time?'

'Nothing,' said the kid.

'Nothing? Well come over here and be useful, you little prick. Jump in and help Jimmy count up this fuckin' change, we're going shopping.'

The van was so hot he felt dizzy. He climbed over the passenger seat and squatted down on the floor in front of the bed where the boy was lying in the same place as the last time he saw him making piles of quarters and dimes and nickels out of a mountain of change that sat on the dirty green sleeping bag beside him. The boy was grey. He didn't look up; he just kept making his piles and humming in a monotone. The kid reached over and scooped up two handfuls and started making his own piles on the sticky shagpile carpet.

They drove south round the bay, heading towards Carmel. The van was set up so the pilot could do everything with his hands. He drove smooth and fast. The kid could see his eyes in the rear-view mirror, they were brown and hard like a hawk's and the skin around them was as puckered and stiff as a crocodile hide. The pilot looked up and caught him staring, their eyes locked and the kid stared straight back without speaking.

'You like my burns, little cowboy?' The kid stayed quiet for a while, then looked down at the change on the floor and started making ten dollar piles.

'I'm a pretty motherfucker, don't ya think?' The kid smiled and kept counting. They pulled into the parking lot of a 24-hour bowling alley next to Longs Drugs and a Burger King. The pilot opened his door and took out a flat board with four wheels bolted to its belly from underneath his seat and dropped it on the ground, then gripped the doorframe with both hands and flung himself out and landed neatly on top of the board.

'Hey, surf's up little fucker, let's go look at some pussy and bring the goddamned shrapnel,' he shouted. Then he began propelling his torso across the parking lot using his arms and hands like they were the oars of a mighty ghost ship.

The Birth Mark

I

They had to be out at seven am, all of them, even the sick. 'I don't know what yer gonna do, maybe get a goddamned job,' said Fat Sally as she filled the mop bucket from the jet spray by the dishwasher, 'but you can't stay here, that's the rules.' It was a long, low basement strung with two flats of fluorescent tube lights that cut bright and hard on the heads of the women as they rolled up the foam mats that they'd been sleeping on. 'Tie 'em up with that string an' throw yer blankets in the corner by the rest room an' take everythang with you, 'cos I'm not responsible fer what ya leave behind. Yeah? It all gets throwed out.'

Fat Sally had been working at the shelter for twenty two years and she loved her girls, every dirty one of them, but she'd learned not to trust even the most holy of angels. 'Rob you in a heartbeat,' she'd say and smile. 'But that's what's been done to them,' nodding her big head slowly up and down, 'one way or another, they all been robbed of something precious, and the crazy thing is, most of them don't even know.'

One by one they came out onto the street, some with

plastic laundry bags in their hands, some with small suit-cases that they dragged behind them on squeaking wheels, others with nothing but loose change held tight in their fists. A young girl with red hair and a big, purple birthmark across the left side of her face sat down on the sidewalk and began tying the laces of her Caterpillar work boots. Next to her a Latina holding a compact mirror in her left hand ran a swath of day-glo pink lipstick over her cracked lips. She pulled her lips together tight with the muscles of her cheeks and made three smacking paps – pap, pap, pap – and arched her eyebrows like Marlene Dietrich as she surveyed the results.

'Bitch, got a cigarette?' she said to the girl sitting on the ground, and the red hair shook slowly from side to side.

'Na, I don't got shit,' said the Latina, 'ain't it the truth?'

'Yeah,' said the redhead, 'you make sure of that.' Then she reached out her hand and grabbed hold of the Latina's and pulled herself slowly to her feet.

They walked arm in arm down Market Street and took a left onto Mission heading towards 16th.

'How comes there ain't no 13th street?' said the redhead as they got to 14th.

''Cos it's bad luck, stupid, even the government knows that,' said the Latina as she turned her head to look at the eyes of the drivers that were passing by. They were close to the zone – the place where things change and the people are more honest about being for sale, by the day, by the hour, by the minute...

'So ya gonna watch my back today?' said the Latina, 'I mean righteously watch my fuckin' back Tina, yeah?' And the redhead nodded and grinned.

'Just don't take so fuckin' long, ok? I get bored when you're gone for a long time an' I just gotta move.'

'Well,' said the Latina, 'I'm gonna be just as quick as I can,' and let go of her arm as a Mexican in a yellow Camaro pulled over on the corner of 15th. She leaned into the window for a moment then stood back, opened the door and climbed in.

II

It's evening, perhaps eight o'clock, in a small back room to the side of the shelter's kitchen. A table, three chairs and a small digital recorder…

'So Teresa, can I ask you some questions?'

'Got a smoke?'

'Yeah.'

He reaches into the bag on the floor by his feet and produces an unopened pack of Marlboro Red. She leans forward on her chair and takes the Marlboro's from his hand and raps the pack of cigarettes on the back of her left hand three times, then uses her teeth to tear off the plastic wrapping and spits it out onto the table and, using her lips, pulls a cigarette out of the pack.

'Got a light?'

'Yeah, sure.'

He reaches into the top pocket of his collared shirt and pulls out a black disposable lighter, which he strikes for her. Teresa reaches up her left arm, puts her hand around his and pulls it over towards her mouth with the cigarette clenched in her front teeth. She holds his hand firmly in hers and stares him in the eye as she pulls on the cigarette.

'Keep the pack,' he says.

'Alrighty, so what do you want to know?'

'Well, how long have you been living on the streets?'

'I don't live on the streets, man, get that straight. Usually we got a hotel room but sometimes we don't so we come down to Sally's 'till we can make up some rent.'

'Well, how do you do that?'

'What?'

'How do you make the money to pay for the hotel?'

'Are you a cop or something? I mean, what the fuck are you askin' me my business for?'

She leans back in her chair, both arms folded across her chest with the cigarette dangling from her mouth. Outside the sound of a drunken argument reaches through the walls, then the sound of a bottle being smashed, and then it gets quiet.

Her name is Teresa, Teresa Arguelo. She's probably in her mid-thirties now. She's been around a long time, used to have an old man, Paco was his name, and they had two kids, but Paco got stabbed to death, must be four years ago now, up in Dolores Park and the kids got put into care and now it's just her and the chiva and crack…

Teresa's got her hair up, up, up, Maria Theresa, La Donna Bonita. Her pale shoulder is sticking out of her denim jacket and her black, toeless stilettos go clickety clickety clack up the sidewalk. Theresa is a tiger; she's striped all over, from the stretch marks ripped onto her belly and her sides that melt into the railroad tracks that climb up her feet and her legs, across her neck and down both arms to her pretty little fingers.

'I ain't no Mexican, I'm a Chicana,' she says. 'I was born right here and I know better than my dumb bean-picking daddy from Sinaloa who worked hard all his life for fuckin' crumbs. All of us know better now, all of us that have been born here, we look at our mamas and papas and say not me baby, uh uh, no way, I'm gonna get mine, one way or another I'm gonna get mine.

'So, mostly I date the Mexicans, yes I do, I date them in their cars and if I get to know them better and they take me back to their apartments or hotel rooms I set 'em up so that Tina can rob them. Tina's a spider, man, she's up those fire escapes, along the edges of the rooftops and down the drain pipes and if I left the window just a little bit open for her that's it, it's all over, that bitch is special, man, she's my whole fuckin' world.'

The door opens and Tina steps into the room holding a can of Coke.

'What's up Ter?'

'Oh, it's cool, this gentleman here jus' wants to ask us some questions and then we get paid.'

'How much?'

'Twenty each.'

'We don't gotta do nothing?'

'Na jus' talk, ain't that right Mr?'

'Yes,' says the man, trying to smile like he's innocent, 'that's right.'

'Well let's do this,' says Tina and pulls up a chair, sits back in it, places her boots on the table by the recorder.

'See this purple stain on my face? Yeah, take a good look, 'cos I'm not ashamed of it, that is a gift from god, do you understand? This purple stain has saved me from being like all those stupid bitches that walk around this world, stupid bitches with their makeup and fuckin' Versace handbags and their husbands who cheat on 'em and their boyfriends who beat on 'em. Shit, I got a tight-ass little body. Look here, don't get shy, see these are some perfect tits – look, ping… ping… And my legs, check this out, my legs, see, like a ballerina or a fuckin' gymnast, and oh, boy, my pussy, my pussy is pink and sweet and always tastes like fresh Bazooka bubble gum baby, don't you worry 'bout that. But this stain is the best part of the package 'cos otherwise I'd be just like Teresa here, a sad beat-up old whore, but it saved me from that shit, man, that and my pride, and don't ask me where that came from 'cos I don't know, I just been born with it, that and my purple fuckin' face.'

The door opens and Sally's big head appears. 'Could you guys wrap it up 'cos I got work to do in here and my girls all gotta be in bed for lights out, ok?'

'Ok,' he says, then looks down at the dictaphone on the plastic table top.

There is silence for a while, then Tina leans forward and places her elbows on the table with her hands rolled up into fists under her chin and stares at him.

'So what are we supposed to tell you? Huh? That we're saving up to get an apartment and go to college? That Teresa here's gonna get her babies back and be a good mom and get a job at Cala Foods? And me? Oh yeah, I'm gonna go and work with disfigured children at the hospital and teach 'em to have some pride and how the world's not such a bad place after all, you just gotta pay income tax and then they'll leave you alone to get on with it. Fuck that, from the age of ten I was fucked on a regular basis by my daddy and his daddy too, huh, motherfucker? Tax payin' motherfuckin' American white males, both of 'em served in the army, patriots right? You know what, I'm fuckin' getting real angry right now. Who the fuck are you, huh? You come down here an' give us a pack of cigarettes and turn on your fuckin' tape recorder an' get us to tell you how it is an' we get fucked up remembering an' then you go get famous with our tragedy like you done something special, you fuckin' fake piece of shit... Come on Teres, we are outta here...'

The door slams, footsteps pounding up the stairs, another door slams, then silence...

The Dirge

God lives in small places, she really does. She lives in holes and cracks that you'd never suspect harboured anything other than cockroaches and dust.

Bonnie and Bill were old for junkies; well, Bill was old and fat from the methadone and the whiskey and the DVTs and Bonnie was about 32, 32 going on 200. The kid had been working for them since he paroled, maybe three months ago now. He slept in their old Pontiac Bonneville outside the hotel on Valencia Street just up from the projects and Bonnie would come down each morning around nine with a thick syringe full of heroin and cocaine and knock on the window to wake him up.

'Hey kid.'

'Hey Bonnie.'

'Did ya sleep ok?'

'Yeah.'

'Good, here's your wake-up an' five bucks for some coffee an' donuts. Come up to the room round about ten and we'll start wrapping.'

'Alright.'

'Alright then.'

'Hey Bonnie?'

'Yeah?'

'Thanks.'

'Ha, no problem kid, when you work for us you get taken care of.'

And he'd lay back down in the backseat of the Bonneville feeling all warm and loved and roll up his right pant leg and push down his sock and tap two fingers against the outside of his ankle where his last snake was sleeping, slide in the needle and wait for a register, then he'd slowly jack the syrup in, stop and pull back on the plunger a bit, wait for that taste to hit the tip of his tongue, close his eyes and drive her home. Then he'd lie back on the seat and raise his leg up into the air so that every little drop could find its way into his heart.

Bonnie came out from Wyoming ten years ago and Bill had been a cowboy in Oklahoma. They'd hooked up in Reno and been together ever since, turning half ounces into a hundred red balloons and running out of veins. Some people can stay in pocket and grind out a living, whereas others just crumble and disappear in the wind. Bill and Bonnie had had a good innings, but now gravity was taking hold and nature was having its never-ending way, because Bill and Bonnie were dying.

At eleven o'clock they'd come out of the hotel and start their rounds. Bill would be up front on his crutches, with his right leg held up fat and yellow and barefoot and covered in crust. He'd wince with every step that he took. Bonnie would be just behind him – eighty eight pounds of HIV skeleton, with her jeans doubled up around a waistline that you could reach around with two hands and the kid keeping up the rear, about twenty yards back with his mouth crammed full of one and ones. Bill and Bonnie had regulars; people who'd been doing business with them for a long time because they knew they were going to get served something with at least a little legs on it, and that was good enough.

The train rolled something like this. The client would tell Bill what was required, then hand the cash to Bonnie who would hold up the appropriate number of fingers behind her back and the kid would spit out the balloons and drop them into the open hand as he passed. Up and down the street, round and round the blocks, 'till everything was sold and it was time to start all over again.

'I can't go back to prison,' said Bill as they waited by the phone box for the half ounces to arrive. 'I won't survive another kick, I just wont fuckin' make it. So if anything goes down you gotta take the rap, can you do that kid?'

'Ah shut up Bill, this is my boy, he knows what to do, don't ya boy?' And looked at the kid with admiration.

'Yeah,' said the kid and looked up the street to see where the cops must be hiding, 'I guess so.'

'Good,' said Bill.

'That's why you're with us you know, it's not 'cos we like you, even though we do, don't we Bonnie?'

And Bonnie said, 'You're like my son.'

'See?' said Bill and the kid nodded his head and felt just a touch embarrassed. 'So do you see?' said Bill again.

'Yeah,' said the kid, 'I fuckin' heard you the first time.'

'Good,' said Bill, ''cos if you don't and I happen to still

be alive somehow, I will kill you, understood?' And Bonnie smiled and put her arm through the kid's and whispered in his ear, 'And if he doesn't, you little motherfucker, I surely will.'

And then she kissed him on the cheek as the delivery man pulled up in his Toyota Corolla with white fake fur on the dashboards and the plastic preying hands of Jesus hanging from the rear-view mirror.

On the bedside table in the dark little box hotel room Bonnie and Bill called home, was a framed photograph of Bill back in the day with an ex-wife and a son, all smiling and in love and American-perfect. 'Forever and ever' was written in black ink on the print beneath the glass. Sometimes at night they'd let the kid come up to the room for a bit and they'd order pizza and ice-cream and then Bill would pass out drinking whiskey laced with methadone and Bonnie would slip forty dollars out of the re-up money in Bill's pocket and go down the hall and buy two rocks. Bill didn't like rocks – he just shot. He said anything else was for amateurs. Bonnie liked smoking rocks, she said it made her feel alive again and when she was smoking she liked to sit on the floor next to the kid while Bill was sleeping and have him give her blowbacks. She would open her mouth wide and place it over his and he would blow all of the smoke out of his lungs into hers then she would hold it a while then lean over and blow it back again into him. She'd keep doing it 'till the smoke was all gone and then she'd put another hit on the pipe and start again.

Bonnie was disappearing right in front of your eyes. Everyday her skin would pull back a little bit more and her teeth and her eyeballs would pop that much further out of her skull, like she was a tide that was rolling back never to return. When Bonnie's mouth was wrapped around the kid's, sometimes he'd think about the virus and he'd try to keep his tongue from touching hers, but then he'd remember that it was probably too late anyway because he'd been stamping her cottons when she wasn't looking and when he found a clogged syringe full of blood and heroin under the bed he'd slipped it in his pocket and fixed it up later in the backseat of the Bonneville, pouring the thick goop out of the back of the barrel into his cooker and mixing it with a bit of whiskey to break it down. When you're gone, you're gone, he figured, so you just get on with it.

On the morning it happened, they all knew it was coming. It had been a rough week, with Bonnie going in and out of the AIDS ward with double pneumonia and her Kaposi sarcoma and malnutrition while Bill had been escaping from the pre-op in a stolen wheelchair two hours before they were due to amputate his right leg at the hip. He had an oxygen tank on his lap and a big plastic mask tied round his face so he could breath as he pushed those wheel rims down 18th Street, stopping every now and then for a Lucky Strike break. Bill had handed the kid the re-up money as he lay on the bed next to Bonnie, trying to get his last breath, and said, 'Well, it's up to you now, we taken care of you good, boy, so don't let us down.' And the kid had nodded his head and taken the money from Bill's yellow hand.

'Bye kid,' said Bonnie.

'Bye Bonnie,' said the kid, and then he closed the door behind him and walked out of the hotel.

The Meteorite

It was the last motel in town, all the way out past the pool hall and the deluxe topless bar and the Union 76 gas station. It sat there on the edge of the desert like a moon base on a dying star, eight little trailers behind a concrete and stucco office and two wooden sheds with showers and toilets, one for gals and one for guys. They had been here for two months now, which was the longest they'd been anywhere in a while. It wasn't like they'd made any decision to stay, they just were tired and wanted to stop driving for a moment. They had six cats living with them in the room, a momma cat and her five kittens. 'No Pets Allowed' said the sign on the front of the sliding glass door of the office, 'Rent to be paid each day in advance, no exceptions.' They were two weeks behind and the only reason they were still there was because the owner's wife loved cats, and she knew they had them in their room because of the smell that hit you when you walked by, that and the fact that she had a soft spot for runaways.

The Ford Bronco II was blue and grey with Washington plates. They had stolen it in Fresno from the parking lot of a bowling alley four months ago. It had just been standing there with the keys hanging out of the driver's side door. They had been pulled over twice since then but nothing had come up when the cops had run the numbers and looked at their fake IDs. Van said they were blessed and that things were gonna change now, Margaret just figured they'd got lucky and that was something you could never count on for long.

In the evenings when the big blue sky turned to pink and the sun settled down behind the San Joaquin mountains, they'd head out in the Bronco for the truck stops that circled Modesto on Route 132 or Highway 99, the freeways going east and west and north and south and all points between. The big semi's lined up next to each other and ran back in rows outside Carl's Junior or Denny's or the big Chevron filling stations. Sometimes the truckers would be sleeping or sometimes they'd be waiting or sometimes they just plain weren't interested.

Van would park up and watch while Margaret did her lipstick in the rear-view mirror, and then she'd tie her shirttails in a bow on top of her stomach, spray on some perfume, light a Salem and step out of the door. When Margaret walked she swayed like a beautiful yacht on the gentle swells of some god given ocean. Van had been with her since she was twelve years old and he was thirteen, and that's just the way it was.

If a truck door opened for her and she stepped up the rungs and disappeared into the cab, Van would give her ten minutes before he went up and knocked on the door. 'Hey mister', he'd say, 'have you seen my little sister? She got long brown hair an' green eyes and my daddy's out here looking for her.' He had a Colt Woodsman .22 semi-automatic pistol with a four-inch barrel and no bullets tucked in the back of his jeans. Usually Margaret was out pretty quick after that and if she wasn't then it was time for plan B.

The night that it happened was like any other except that they'd seen a shooting star as they drove out to work. Margaret had grabbed Van's hand on the steering wheel and said, 'Make a wish, make a wish,' but Van couldn't think of anything so he just pretended he had. When they got to the stop they saw a big white Peterbilt with Missouri plates sitting by itself on the edge of the lot. It looked brand spanking new and Margaret had got out of the Bronco and walked over to the cab, stepped up the rungs and knocked on the window and then Van watched as she opened the door and stepped inside. Van leaned back in the driver's seat and lit a Camel, put on the radio and closed his eyes, listening to Hank Williams singing about honky tonkin' round this town and when he opened his eyes at the end of the song the truck was gone. 'Motherfucker,' said Van and turned over the engine and jammed his boot on the gas and peeled the Bronco out to the 99 on ramps. 'North or south?' he said to himself. South you had to go under the bridge and back around; north was straight ahead. 'North or south, sweet Jesus,' Van said again, and then he remembered watching the tail of the shooting star running up the sky due north towards Oregon and Margaret's hand clutching his on the steering wheel as she whispered her secret to whatever god might be interested, and so that's the way that he went.

The Virgin

'Paul, Paul?'

'What?' shouted Paul.

'Who's here?' said his mother from her bedroom.

'Nobody, you dumb bitch,' said Paul as he finished rolling a joint on the coffee table in the dirty living room.

'Paul, I don't want nobody in my house, you hear me?'

'Yeah, yeah, yeah,' said Paul, and lit the joint and took a hit, then passed it on to his buddy Jeff who was sitting next to him on the couch with Carolee Pewthers perched on top of his knees. Jeff took the joint, placed it into his lips and inhaled, then reached his hand up and pulled back Carolee's long brown hair and placed his mouth over hers and blew all the smoke from his lungs into hers and when it was gone he followed it with his tongue.

'Paul?' said his mother, who was now standing in the hallway with one hand on the wall to hold her steady. She was skinny and old looking with a swollen belly and red-rimmed eyelids that circled two yellow orbs that leaked something wet down her veined cheeks. 'Paul?' she said again like glass being scraped with a blade and she staggered into the living room with her right hand raised and her finger pointed in the direction of the kids on her couch. 'Gedum the fuck outta here, Paul,' she said and then clenched her fingers into a fist that hung shaking and uncertain in the smoke-filled air. 'Get dese people outta my house right now, d'ya hear me? Paul? Paul?'

Carolee Pewthers was fourteen years old and she was smart and pretty and had had a boyfriend for two years now, who was smart like her, smart and athletic and a good guy. Carolee's family was moving to Sacramento in two weeks and Carolee had decided that she wanted to lose her virginity before she moved. It just seemed like the grown up thing to do, but she didn't want to lose it to her boyfriend, she wanted to lose it to Jeff Acosta.

When she rang the doorbell of Paul Douglas's house at ten am on Sunday morning her family was at church. She had said, 'Mom, I'm not feeling too good,' and her mom had said, 'Ok honey, you just stay in bed and get better,' and kissed her on the forehead, and when she'd closed the front door and Carolee had heard their car pull out of the garage, she jumped up and brushed her hair and put on some light pink lipstick and a new pair of panties and a little white cotton dress that showed off her pretty brown legs. As she stood in front of her bedroom mirror she tried to remember why she was doing this, she closed her eyes and placed her hand on her stomach and gently ran her fingers up to her breast, she traced a circle around her nipple and then squeezed her breast real hard in her fist, rubbing it up and down and listening in her head to the sounds she'd heard coming out of her parents' room late at night.

'Hey,' said Jeff when he opened the door. 'Hey,' said Carolee and held out the small bottle of Southern Comfort she'd stolen from her dad's liquor cabinet. 'Cool,' said Jeff as he reached over and pulled her by the wrist into the hallway and kissed her up against the wall, putting his hands on her breasts and squeezing them just the way he was supposed to.

Paul Douglas's mom was an alcoholic. For the past two years she had been in and out of the Crystal Springs rehabilitation hospital and Paul had been left to fend for himself as the house fell apart and the bills piled up in unopened letters strewn across the kitchen table. Sometimes the electricity would be off for a week or more until Paul's father showed up and kicked Paul's ass and paid the bills and disappeared again.

When she was home Paul's mom didn't leave the bedroom, she didn't eat or make meals or have showers or go shopping or tidy the house or anything, she just had liquor delivered and chain-smoked Pall Malls until she started haemorrhaging again and Paul would have to call the ambulance.

'Paul? Paul?' Paul got off the couch and picked up an ashtray and threw it at the wall next to his mother's head where it exploded like fireworks in a fourth of July sky. 'Shut up, you dumb bitch!' he yelled and closed in on her with his hands clenched together in two fists and his wire frame glasses perched sideways on his zit-covered nose. 'Shut up and get the fuck back in your room you drunk fuckin' bitch, I fuckin' hate your guts, you useless fuckin' whore.' And Paul's mother raised her skinny arms up to cover her face and started wailing as Paul's fists rained down in weak little drops of poison upon the sides of her head.

'Oh my god,' said Carolee, pushing Jeff's hand out from between her legs, 'oh my god, he's hitting his mother, do something!' and she jumped up from the couch with her hand covering her mouth as Paul dragged his mother by the hair down the hallway and back into her bedroom. 'Don't worry about it, baby,' said Jeff, standing up and stroking her soft, brown cheeks. He took the joint from his teeth and put it in between her lips and Carolee took a little hit and the room started spinning around and Jeff pushed her up against the living room wall and started kissing her neck and pulling down her new panties at the same time.

At first when he put it in her it had hurt and she had made a little wincing sound and bitten her lip but then Jeff pulled it out and spat on his hand and rubbed it all around its end and put it back gently and she had sighed and placed her hands on top of his shoulders and then it had felt real nice and warm and Jeff had picked up her legs in his arms and he was holding her up against the wall and this was it. He was pushing it in and out and in and out and she felt like she was swimming in a warm pool of velvet, and when she opened her eyes and caught a glimpse of Paul, who was sitting on the couch with his jeans round his knees watching them and jerking off his little white cock at the same time, she'd thought for a moment that something was wrong, but then she'd just closed her eyes again and for a moment she swore she could hear the angels singing sweeter than any church choir that she had ever heard.

The Kids

It was a 1975 Ford LTD station wagon, bright yellow with a 400ci engine, no gas and two flat tires. It had been parked up on Shotwell and 14th Street for six nights now. In the back seat two little boys lay curled up asleep, the little one had his thumb in his mouth and the older boy had dropped off holding a McDonald's milkshake in his hand. There was a small pool of chocolate that had leaked out of the straw and onto the seat. The floor was covered in trash and dirty clothes and empty forty-ounce bottles of Schlitz malt liquor. A plastic rosary hung from the rear-view mirror, the tip of the small white crucifix stained brown from where it had been used to break down heroin in the bottle cap cooker that sat on the floor underneath the driver's seat.

You could tell they were brothers, part Mexican maybe, with the same brown eyes and long lashes and dirty brown hair. Up until last week they'd been in a care home for six months, their mother had had a visit scheduled last Saturday morning and she'd shown up with their father who'd just been released from county jail. They were supposed to go to the zoo and be back for six o'clock that evening but one thing led to another and before you know it had been six days and now everything had changed.

The little one was the first to wake up and he kicked out his foot where his brother had been laying on it in the back seat of the station wagon.

'Move,' he said and his brother opened his eyes then closed them again. 'Where's mom?'

'I don't know, she's not back yet an' if you kick me again I'm gonna punch you in the face.'

'But you were layin' on my foot.'

'I don't care, so shut up.'

'Davey?'

'What?' said the older one.

'I gotta pee.'

'Well then, go pee.'

'Davey?'

'What?'

'Come with me.'

'Oh Jesus, you're such a fuckin' baby,' said the older one and then he pushed open the back door of the LTD and they stepped out onto the pavement in their bare feet.

Their mom and dad had been together on and off for ten years now. Lisa had little blue tears tattooed underneath the outsides of both of her eyes and an upside down cross made from two wavy lines that she'd done herself when she was fifteen sat in the middle of her forehead.

George knew that his oldest boy was really his brother Ron's, but he never said anything. He was a good kid and so was little Davey. The kids had grown up watching him fix, he did everything with them, just like now when they were up against it and Lisa sometimes had to bring tricks back to the car, she'd just cover the kids up with a blanket and take care of business in the front seat. She tried to not make too much noise but sometimes they'd wake up and she'd say, 'Hush, go back to sleep.' Lisa had started giving them little bits of her methadone in their soda at night, it seemed to help them sleep and they didn't wake up so much. Just a little, she thought, it can't do no harm, and the kids had felt all warm and safe, for a while.

Lisa had a broken back – she'd fallen off the roof of a warehouse on Army Street after smoking so much crack that she lost the ability to tell up from down. She'd been in SF General for three months and had just started to walk again using crutches. The boys had been at George's mom's when it happened, but she worked full-time and when Lisa's doctors called from the hospital to tell her where Lisa was, she'd snapped. 'I can't fuckin' do it. George is in jail and she's running round the streets every night and I can't cope. The kids are great, but I just can't do it.' And later that day the lady from children's welfare had patted her on the hand and held out a pen for her to sign the paperwork.

'I didn't jump goddamn it, I fell!' Lisa yelled at the social worker who was investigating their case.

'But what were you doing on the roof of an abandoned building at two in the morning Lisa?'

'I was counting the stars.'

'Twenty miles away from your kids?'

'They were with their grandma.'

'She's not their mother, Lisa, she's old and not well herself and has a full-time job and has been through a lot, raising her own two sons, as you should know. Now

George is in jail and you're really struggling, have you thought about going to rehab, Lisa?'

'Oh fuck,' said Lisa and grabbed her crutches from where they were leaning against the chair in the office of the California Department of Child Welfare.

When George got released from county last Saturday morning after serving nine months for two petty thefts, he'd wanted to do the right thing with all of his heart, he really did, but as soon as they got into San Francisco in his mom's car and had picked up the kids and they were heading to the zoo, Lisa had said, 'Come on George, just one speedball and we'll go. George I got a hundred bucks… George? George?'

'You got to make some money, George,' said Lisa after they got back to the car and fixed. The kids were sitting quietly, waiting to see if there was going to be any food.'

'I'm hungry mom,' said Davey.

'Shut up,' said Lisa and George just rubbed his nose and stuck his two front teeth out on top of his bottom lip and just kind of froze there.

'George you look like a fuckin' rabbit,' said Lisa. 'Look at you, you're fuckin' useless! You're a fuckin' pussy, George. Oh fuck, I wish Ron was here, he'd know how to get us some money, George? Can you hear me George?' And George just kind of rocked there rubbing his nose with his thumb, hoping that she would just go and do another trick and leave him alone.

'George, if you don't go and make some money I'm leaving you and the kids and I'm fuckin' gone, do you hear me? George, George! I got a broken back for Christ's sake,

George, and I'm doing ten-dollar tricks and you ain't doin' nothing but following me round like a fuckin' puppy dog waitin' to do the dope an' the kids need to eat, George, an' I swear to god I ain't givin' you no more of the drugs, George, not even a cotton. George do you hear me?'

'Yes Lisa,' said George, 'I hear you.'

George stood on the sidewalk outside the Wells Fargo bank on Market and Dolores. He was breathing fast and little tears of sweat rolled down the sides of his forehead and into his eyes. The kids were on a bench across the street – he'd told them to wait and bought them a cherry Coke and a small bag of Doritos. He had a note in one pocket of his black trench coat and a brown paper bag that covered a screwdriver he was holding in his right hand stuck deep in the other pocket. The note said, 'Please give me all your money and don't say anything, I have a gun and I'll shoot you if you don't help me. Thank you.' He'd almost signed his name after 'thank you', but then he caught himself. 'I'm fuckin' scared. I've always been scared, oh shit,' he said out loud, then punched himself in the face like Ron used to do to get him angry, and walked into the bank.

The Mummy

It's gotta be almost over, I thought. Please god, if you even got a set of ears, hear me now. I was laying on two cardboard flats on some grass behind a white stucco wall across the street from Dolores Park, I didn't have a blanket or sleeping bag, just my stealing jacket and I remember trying to hug my knees up into my stomach because it was so fucking cold and George wasn't going to be there 'till nine or ten in the morning, or whenever he could manage to get a car for us to operate in. Being cold and trying to sleep don't go together very well, especially if you're not full of heroin. It's like life is that much harder without drugs, everything is magnified and you're easy prey for bumps and bruises and the understanding's pretty clear that you have become a nobody-nothing kind of animal sub-thing that walks and talks in perpetual lies and angles that are all meant to hook a hit somehow. Everything is gauged on getting that hit.

Back then everyone in the Mission was fucked up in some way, I mean really fucked up and broken and leaking gas all down the freeway. I heard that now they cleaned it all up and normal people who have jobs and money have taken over, but it wasn't always that way – then it was the refuse pile for America's trash. I wonder where they have all gone to now.

Well I'm gonna tell you a little tale. Let's say that was the morning that George never showed, that was the morning I had to set off on my two stinking feet looking for carrion and diamonds and ended up outside this little bungalow behind a block of apartments on Van Ness near 21st and happened to notice that the mailbox on the front door was stuffed to overflowing. Bing! Light bulb, nobody's home and it's been that way for a while, so I walk round the side and jimmy a window that's crumbling with age. Up goes the window and in goes my wretched soul attached to what's left of my skin and bones.

It's dark in the bungalow, real dark and it smells bad. I hit a switch and nothing, no juice, no electricity, no life. I can just make out a TV set and a stereo and some dresser drawers and I get to work and unplug the TV and make a pile with the pioneer stereo. Then I turn round to look for some blankets or sheets to wrap the goodies up in and there in the bed is the dim outline of somebody laying still as still can be. For a moment I froze and watched real careful. It didn't move. In fact, I realised that it wasn't even breathing; it was just there...

'Hello,' I said.

Nothing.

'Hello there Mr,' I said again.

Nada.

So I edge on over to the bed and get the full view of what it is before me.

Old. It's old and bald and kinda frozen there with one arm over its head covering his eyes and on the end of the arm by the hand is a silver wristwatch. I remember reaching out slowly and touching the arm. Stiff. Stiff and cold and dead. I pulled the arm down, which was kind of weird because it was stuck in place and for a moment it was like we were wrist-wrestling, but I managed and lo, there's a gold ring on one of his fingers and nobody but me and him to be seen, and him being dead kind of put all the odds in my favour, so off comes the watch, but the ring wouldn't budge. I had to spit on my fingers and work it into his skin awhile and spin and twist and spin and pop, I go' ya.

I stood back for a moment and wondered about his teeth. No, I thought, I'm not gonna pull out any gold teeth even if there are any sitting in this poor old man's jaw. So, he is bald as a chestnut, shiny and sucked up and kind of looks like a spider caught dead in its own web. Husk-like, I guess. Just the sheath and no meat or life, in fact, he looked like a mummy from some sad pyramid. What you doing here dead Mr, I thought. How come the mailbox is full and nobody gives a fuck and you've probably been here about a week and not a soul has seemed to miss you. In fact, you could be me, I realised. Yes, we have something in common, but I earned my fate. I wonder what you did to be of no consequence or meaning to anybody else in the world.

But, you know, there were things to be done and shekels to be made and I certainly didn't want to be the only fellow in town in case the ambulance arrived, so I wrapped up the gear in a blanket like it was Santa's bag, woop, over my shoulder with the ring and the watch in my pocket and clambered back out the window and headed down Vann Ness to Hunt's Donuts feeling just that little bit smaller than I had when I'd first woken up in the morning.

Chris Wilson was born in 1961 in Newcastle-upon-Tyne, England and grew up in Dar es Salaam, East Africa. He moved with his parents to California in 1971. After many years of living in the streets and prisons of the USA, he was extradited to the UK in 1998. Since becoming drug and crime free in 2001, he has studied at the Chelsea College of Art and Design, where he was awarded a First with Distinction. His paintings have been exhibited across the UK and his first book, *Horse Latitudes*, was published in 2013. He currently lives in London.

August 2016

This first edition is published as a

trade paperback; there are 126 numbered

& lettered copies signed by the author, & handbound

in boards by the Tangerine Press, Tooting, London;

lettered copies also contain an original

painting by Chris Wilson.